The Spy Who Came
In From the Cold

The Spy Who Came In From the Cold

✠

John le Carré

Coward-McCann, Inc.
New York

The Spy Who Came
In From the Cold

✠ ✠ 1 ✠ Checkpoint

The American handed Leamas another cup of coffee and said, "Why don't you go back and sleep? We can ring you if he shows up."

Leamas said nothing, just stared through the window of the checkpoint, along the empty street.

"You can't wait forever, sir. Maybe he'll come some other time. We can have the *Polizei* contact the Agency: you can be back here in twenty minutes."

"No," said Leamas, "it's nearly dark now."

"But you can't wait forever; he's nine hours over schedule."

"If you want to go, go. You've been very good," Leamas added. "I'll tell Kramer you've been damn good."

"But how long will you wait?"

"Until he comes." Leamas walked to the observation window and stood between the two motionless policemen. Their binoculars were trained on the Eastern checkpoint.

"He's waiting for the dark," Leamas muttered, "I know he is."

"This morning you said he'd come across with the workmen."

Leamas turned on him.

"Agents aren't airplanes. They don't have schedules. He's blown, he's on the run, he's frightened. Mundt's after him, now, at this moment. He's got only one chance. Let him choose his time."

The younger man hesitated, wanting to go and not finding the moment.

A bell rang inside the hut. They waited, suddenly alert. A policeman said in German, "Black Opel Rekord, Federal registration."

"He can't see that far in the dusk, he's guessing," the American whispered and then he added: "How did Mundt know?"

"Shut up," said Leamas from the window.

One of the policemen left the hut and walked to the sandbag emplacement two feet short of the white demarkation which lay across the road like the base line of a tennis court. The other waited until his companion was crouched behind the telescope in the emplacement, then put down his binoculars, took his black helmet from the peg by the door and carefully adjusted it on his head. Somewhere high above the checkpoint the arclights sprang to life, casting theatrical beams onto the road in front of them.

The policeman began his commentary. Leamas knew it by heart.

"Car halts at the first control. Only one oecupant, a woman. Escorted to the Vopo hut for document check." They waited in silence.

"What's he saying?" said the American. Leamas didn't reply. Picking up a spare pair of binoculars, he gazed fixedly toward the East German controls.

"Document check completed. Admitted to the second control."

"Mr. Leamas, is this your man?" the American persisted. "I ought to ring the Agency."

"Wait."

"Where's the car now? What's it doing?"

"Currency check, Customs," Leamas snapped.

Leamas watched the car. There were two Vopos at the driver's door, one doing the talking, the other standing off, waiting. A third was sauntering around the car. He stopped at the trunk, then walked back to the driver. He wanted the key. He opened the trunk, looked inside, closed it, returned the key and walked thirty yards up the road to where, midway between the two opposing checkpoints, a solitary East German sentry was standing, a squat silhouette in boots and baggy trousers. The two stood together talking, self-conscious in the glare of the arclight.

With a perfunctory gesture they waved the car on. It reached the two sentries in the middle of the road and stopped again. They walked around the car, stood off and talked again; finally, almost unwillingly, they let it continue across the line to the Western sector.

"It is a man you're waiting for, Mr. Leamas?" asked the American.

"Yes, it's a man."

Pushing up the collar of his jacket, Leamas stepped outside into the icy October wind. He remembered the crowd then. It was something you forgot inside the hut, this group of puzzled faces. The people changed but the expressions were the same. It was like the helpless crowd that gathers around a traffic accident, no one knowing how it happened, whether you should move the body. Smoke or dust rose through the beams of the arc lamps, a constant shifting pall between the margins of light.

Leamas walked over to the car and said to the woman, "Where is he?"

"They came for him and he ran. He took the bicycle. They can't have known about me."

"Where did he go?"

"We had a room near Brandenburg, over a pub. He kept a few things there, money, papers. I think he'll have gone there. Then he'll come over."

"Tonight?"

"He said he would come tonight. The others have all been caught—Paul, Viereck, Ländser, Salomon. He hasn't got long."

Leamas stared at her for a moment in silence.

"Ländser too?"

"Last night."

A policeman was standing at Leamas' side.

"You'll have to move away from here," he said. "It's forbidden to obstruct the crossing point."

Leamas half turned. "Go to hell," he snapped.

The German stiffened, but the woman said, "Get in. We'll drive down to the corner."

He got in beside her and they drove slowly until they reached a side road.

"I didn't know you had a car," he said.

"It's my husband's," she replied indifferently. "Karl never told you I was married, did he?" Leamas was silent. "My husband and I work for an optical firm. They let us over to do business. Karl only told you my maiden name. He didn't want me to be mixed up with . . . you."

Leamas took a key from his pocket.

"You'll want somewhere to stay," he said. His voice

sounded flat. "There's an apartment in the Albrecht-Dürer-Strasse, next to the Museum. Number 28A. You'll find everything you want. I'll telephone you when he comes."

"I'll stay here with you."

"I'm not staying here. Go to the flat. I'll ring you. There's no point in waiting here now."

"But he's coming to this crossing point."

Leamas looked at her in surprise.

"He told you that?"

"Yes. He knows one of the Vopos there, the son of his landlord. It may help. That's why he chose this route."

"And he told *you* that?"

"He trusts me. He told me everything."

"Christ."

He gave her the key and went back to the checkpoint hut, out of the cold. The policemen were muttering to each other as he entered; the larger one ostentatiously turned his back.

"I'm sorry," said Leamas. "I'm sorry I bawled you out." He opened a tattered briefcase and rummaged in it until he found what he was looking for: a half bottle of whisky. With a nod the elder man accepted it, half filled each coffee mug and topped them up with black coffee.

"Where's the American gone?" asked Leamas.

"Who?"

"The CIA boy. The one who was with me."

"Bedtime," said the elder man and they all laughed.

Leamas put down his mug and said, "What are your rules for shooting to protect a man coming over? A man on the run."

"We can only give covering fire if the Vopos shoot into our sector."

"That means you can't shoot until a man's over the boundary?"

The older man said, "We can't give covering fire, Mr. . . ."

"Thomas," Leamas replied. "Thomas." They shook hands, the two policemen pronouncing their own names as they did so.

"We can't give covering fire. That's the truth. They tell us there'd be war if we did."

"It's nonsense," said the younger policeman, emboldened by the whisky. "If the allies weren't here the Wall would be gone by now."

"So would Berlin," muttered the elder man.

"I've got a man coming over tonight," said Leamas abruptly.

"Here? At this crossing point?"

"It's worth a lot to get him out. Mundt's men are looking for him."

"There are still places where you can climb," said the younger policeman.

"He's not that kind. He'll bluff his way through; he's got papers, if the papers are still good. He's got a bicycle."

There was only one light in the checkpoint, a reading lamp with a green shade, but the glow of the arclights, like artificial moonlight, filled the cabin. Darkness had fallen, and with it silence. They spoke as if they were afraid of being overheard. Leamas went to the window and waited, in front of him the road and to either side the Wall, a dirty, ugly thing of breeze blocks and strands of barbed wire, lit with cheap yellow light, like the backdrop for a concentration camp. East and west of the Wall lay the unrestored part of Berlin, a half-world of ruin, drawn in two dimensions, crags of war.

That damned woman, thought Leamas, and that fool Karl,

who'd lied about her. Lied by omission, as they all do, agents the world over. You teach them to cheat, to cover their tracks, and they cheat you as well. He'd only produced her once, after that dinner in the Schürzstrasse last year. Karl had just had his big scoop and Control had wanted to meet him. Control always came in on success. They'd had dinner together—Leamas, Control and Karl. Karl loved that kind of thing. He turned up looking like a Sunday school boy, scrubbed and shining, doffing his hat and all respectful.

Control had shaken his hand for five minutes and said: "I want you to know how pleased we are, Karl, damn pleased." Leamas had watched and thought, That'll cost us another couple of hundred a year.

When they'd finished dinner Control pumped their hands again, nodded significantly and, implying that he had to go off and risk his life somewhere else, got back into his chauffeur-driven car. Then Karl had laughed, and Leamas had laughed with him, and they'd finished the champagne, still laughing about Control. Afterwards they'd gone to the Alter Fass; Karl had insisted on it and there Elvira was waiting for them, a forty-year-old blonde, tough as nails.

"This is my best kept secret, Alec," Karl had said, and Leamas was furious. Afterwards they'd had a row.

"How much does she know? Who is she? How did you meet her?" Karl sulked and refused to say. After that things went badly. Leamas tried to alter the routine, change the meeting places and the catchwords, but Karl didn't like it. He knew what lay behind it and he didn't like it.

"If you don't trust her it's too late anyway," he'd said, and Leamas took the hint and shut up. But he went carefully after that, told Karl much less, used more of the hocus-pocus of espionage technique. And there she was, out there in her car, knowing everything, the whole network, the safe house, everything; and Leamas swore, not for the first time, never to trust an agent again.

He went to the telephone and dialed the number of his flat. Frau Martha answered.

"We've got guests at the Dürer Strasse," said Leamas, "a man and a woman."

"Married?" asked Martha.

"Near enough," said Leamas, and she laughed that frightful laugh. As he put down the receiver one of the policemen turned to him.

"Herr Thomas! Quick!" Leamas stepped to the observation window.

"A man, Herr Thomas," the younger policeman whispered, "with a bicycle." Leamas picked up the binoculars.

It was Karl, the figure was unmistakable even at that distance, shrouded in an old Wehrmacht mackintosh, pushing his bicycle. He's made it, thought Leamas, he must have made it, he's through the document check, only currency and customs to go. Leamas watched Karl lean his bicycle against the railing, walk casually to the customs hut. Don't overdo it, he thought. At last Karl came out, waved cheerfully to the man on the barrier, and the red and white pole swung slowly upwards. He was through, he was coming toward them, he had made it. Only the Vopo in the middle of the road, the line and safety.

At that moment Karl seemed to hear some sound, sense some danger; he glanced over his shoulder, began to pedal furiously, bending low over the handlebars. There was still the lonely sentry on the bridge, and he had turned and was watching Karl. Then, totally unexpected, the searchlights went on, white and brilliant, catching Karl and holding him in their beam like a rabbit in the headlights of a car. There came the seesaw wail of a siren, the sound of orders wildly shouted. In front of Leamas the two policemen dropped to their knees, peering through the sandbagged slits, deftly flicking the rapid load on their automatic rifles.

The East German sentry fired, quite carefully, away from them, into his own sector. The first shot seemed to thrust Karl forward, the second to pull him back. Somehow he was still moving, still on the bicycle, passing the sentry, and the sentry was still shooting at him. Then he sagged, rolled to the ground, and they heard quite clearly the clatter of the bike as it fell. Leamas hoped to God he was dead.

✠ ✠ 2 ✠ The Circus

He watched the Templehof runway sink beneath him.

Leamas was not a reflective man and not a particularly philosophical one. He knew he was written off—it was a fact of life which he would henceforth live with, as a man must live with cancer or imprisonment. He knew there was no kind of preparation which could have bridged the gap between then and now. He met failure as one day he would probably meet death, with cynical resentment and the courage of a solitary. He'd lasted longer than most; now he was beaten. It is said a dog lives as long as its teeth; metaphorically, Leamas' teeth had been drawn; and it was Mundt who had drawn them.

Ten years ago he could have taken the other path—there were desk jobs in that anonymous government building in Cambridge Circus which Leamas could have taken and kept till he was God knows how old; but Leamas wasn't made that way. You might as well have asked a jockey to become a bet-ting clerk as expect Leamas to abandon operational life for the tendentious theorizing and clandestine self-interest of Whitehall. He had stayed on in Berlin, conscious that Personnel had marked his file for review at the end of every year —stubborn, willful, contemptuous of instruction, telling himself that something would turn up. Intelligence work has one moral law—it is justified by results. Even the sophistry of Whitehall paid court to that law, and Leamas got results. Until Mundt came.

It was odd how soon Leamas had realized that Mundt was the writing on the wall.

Hans-Dieter Mundt, born forty-two years ago in Leipzig. Leamas knew his dossier, knew the photograph on the inside of the cover, the blank, hard face beneath the flaxen hair; knew by heart the story of Mundt's rise to power as second man in the Abteilung and effective head of operations. Mundt was hated even within his own department. Leamas knew that from the evidence of defectors, and from Riemeck, who as a member of the SED Praesidium sat on security committees with Mundt, and dreaded him. Rightly as it turned out, for Mundt had killed him.

Until 1959 Mundt had been a minor functionary of the Abteilung, operating in London under the cover of the East German Steel Mission. He returned to Germany in a hurry after murdering two of his own agents to save his skin and was not heard of for more than a year. Quite suddenly he reappeared at the Abteilung's headquarters in Leipzig as head of the Ways and Means Department, responsible for allocating currency, equipment and personnel for special tasks. At the end of that year came the big struggle for power within the Abteilung. The number and influence of Soviet liaison officers were drastically reduced, several of the old guard were dismissed on ideological grounds and three men emerged: Fiedler as head of counterintelligence, Jahn took over from Mundt as head of facilities, and Mundt himself got the plum—deputy director of operations—at the age of forty-one. Then the new style began. The first agent Leamas lost was a girl. She was only a small link in the network; she was used for courier jobs. They shot her dead in the street as she left a West Berlin cinema. The police never found the murderer and Leamas was at first inclined to write the incident off as unconnected with her work. A month later a railroad porter in Dresden, a discarded agent from Peter Guillam's network, was found dead and mutilated beside a railroad track. Leamas knew it wasn't coincidence any longer. Soon after that two members of another network under Leamas' control were arrested and summarily sentenced to death. So it went on: remorseless and unnerving.

And now they had Karl, and Leamas was leaving Berlin as he had come—without a single agent worth a farthing. Mundt had won.

Leamas was a short man with close-cropped, iron-gray hair, and the physique of a swimmer. He was very strong. This strength was discernible in his back and shoulders, in his neck, and in the stubby formation of his hands and fingers.

He had a utilitarian approach to clothes, as he did to most other things, and even the spectacles he occasionally wore had steel rims. Most of his suits were of artificial fiber, none of them had waistcoats. He favored shirts of the American kind with buttons on the points of the collars, and suede shoes with rubber soles.

He had an attractive face, muscular, and a stubborn line

to his thin mouth. His eyes were brown and small; Irish, some said. It was hard to place Leamas. If he were to walk into a London club the porter would certainly not mistake him for a member; in a Berlin night club they usually gave him the best table. He looked like a man who could make trouble, a man who looked after his money; a man who was not quite a gentleman.

The stewardess thought he was interesting. She guessed that he was North of England, which he might well have been, and rich, which he was not. She put his age at fifty, which was about right. She guessed he was single, which was half true. Somewhere long ago there had been a divorce; somewhere there were children, now in their teens, who received their allowance from a rather odd private bank in the City.

"If you want another whisky," said the stewardess, "you'd better hurry. We shall be at London airport in twenty minutes."

"No more." He didn't look at her; he was looking out of the window at the gray-green fields of Kent.

Fawley met him at the airport and drove him to London.

"Control's pretty cross about Karl," he said, looking sideways at Leamas. Leamas nodded.

"How did it happen?" asked Fawley.

"He was shot. Mundt got him."

"Dead?"

"I should think so, by now. He'd better be. He nearly made it. He should never have hurried, they couldn't have been sure. The Abteilung got to the checkpoint just after he'd been let through. They started the siren and a Vopo shot him twenty yards short of the line. He moved on the ground for a moment, then lay still."

"Poor bastard."

"Precisely," said Leamas.

Fawley didn't like Leamas, and if Leamas knew he didn't care. Fawley was a man who belonged to clubs and wore representative ties, pontificated on the skills of sportsmen and assumed a service rank in office correspondence. He thought Leamas suspect, and Leamas thought him a fool.

"What section are you in?" asked Leamas.

"Personnel."

"Like it?"

"Fascinating."

"Where do I go now? On ice?"

"Better let Control tell you, old boy."

"Do you know?"

"Of course."

"Then why the hell don't you tell me?"

"Sorry, old man," Fawley replied, and Leamas suddenly very nearly lost his temper. Then he reflected that Fawley was probably lying anyway.

"Well, tell me one thing, do you mind? Have I got to look for a bloody flat in London?"

Fawley scratched at his ear: "I don't think so, old man, no."

"No? Thank God for that."

They parked near Cambridge Circus, at a parking meter, and went together into the hall.

"You haven't got a pass, have you? You'd better fill in a slip, old man."

"Since when have we had passes? McCall knows me as well as his own mother."

"Just a new routine. Circus is growing, you know."

Leamas said nothing, nodded at McCall and got into the lift without a pass.

Control shook his hand rather carefully, like a doctor feeling the bones.

"You must be awfully tired," he said apologetically, "do sit down." That same dreary voice, the donnish bray.

Leamas sat down in a chair facing an olive-green electric fire with a bowl of water balanced on the top of it.

"Do you find it cold?" Control asked. He was stooping over the fire rubbing his hands together. He wore a cardigan under his black jacket, a shabby brown one. Leamas remembered Control's wife, a stupid little woman called Mandy who seemed to think her husband was on the Coal Board. He supposed she had knitted it.

"It's so dry, that's the trouble." Control continued. "Beat the cold and you parch the atmosphere. Just as dangerous." He went to the desk and pressed some button. "We'll try and get some coffee," he said. "Ginnie's on leave, that's the trouble. They've given me some new girl. It really is too bad." He was shorter than Leamas remembered him; otherwise, just the same. The same affected detachment, the same fusty conceits; the same horror of drafts; courteous according to a formula miles removed from Leamas' experience. The same milk-and-water smile, the same elaborate diffidence, the same apologetic adherence to a code of behavior which he pretended to find ridiculous. The same banality.

He brought a pack of cigarettes from the desk and gave one to Leamas.

"You're going to find these more expensive," he said and Leamas nodded dutifully. Slipping the cigarettes into his pocket, Control sat down.

There was a pause; finally Leamas said: "Riemeck's dead."

"Yes, indeed," Control declared, as if Leamas had made a good point. "It is very unfortunate. Most. . . . I suppose that girl blew him—Elvira?"

"I suppose so." Leamas wasn't going to ask him how he knew about Elvira.

"And Mundt had him shot," Control added.

"Yes."

Control got up and drifted around the room looking for an ashtray. He found one and put it awkwardly on the floor between their two chairs.

"How did you feel? When Riemeck was shot, I mean? You saw it, didn't you?"

Leamas shrugged. "I was bloody annoyed," he said.

Control put his head to one side and half closed his eyes. "Surely you felt more than that? Surely you were upset? That would be more natural."

"I was upset. Who wouldn't be?"

"Did you like Riemeck—as a man?"

"I suppose so," said Leamas helplessly. "There doesn't seem much point in going into it," he added.

"How did you spend the night, what was left of it, after Riemeck had been shot?"

"Look, what is this?" Leamas asked hotly; "what are you getting at?"

"Riemeck was the last," Control reflected, "the last of a series of deaths. If my memory is right it began with the girl, the one they shot in Wedding, outside the cinema. Then there was the Dresden man, and the arrests at Jena. Like the ten little niggers. Now Paul, Viereck .ndLändser—all dead. And finally Riemeck." He smiled deprecatingly. "That is quite a heavy rate of expenditure. I wondered if you'd had enough."

"What do you mean—enough?"

"I wondered whether you w ,re tired. Burned out." There was ' long silence.

"That s up to you," I amas said at last.

"We have to live without sympathy, don't we? That's impossible of course. We act it to one another, all this hardness; but we aren't like that really. I mean . . . one can't be out in the cold all the time; one has to come in from the cold . . . do you see what I mean?"

Leamas saw. He saw the long road outside Rotterdam, the long straight road beside the dunes, and the stream of refugees moving along it; saw the little airplane miles away, the procession stop and look toward it; and the plane coming in, neatly over the dunes; saw the chaos, the meaningless hell, as the bombs hit the road.

"I can't talk like this, Control," Leamas said at last. "What do you want me to do?"

"I want you to stay out in the cold a little longer." Leamas said nothing, so Control went on: "The ethic of our work, as I understand it, is based on a single assumption. That is, we are never going to be aggressors. Do you think that's fair?"

Leamas nodded. Anything to avoid talking.

"Thus we do disagreeable things, but we are *defensive*. That, I think, is still fair. We do disagreeable things so that ordinary people here and elsewhere can sleep safely in their beds at night. Is that too romantic? Of course, we occasionally do very wicked things." He grinned like a schoolboy.

"And in weighing up the moralities, we rather go in for dishonest comparisons; after all, you can't compare the ideals of one side with the methods of the other, can you now?"

Leamas was lost. He'd heard the man talked a lot of drivel before getting the knife in, but he'd never heard anything like this before.

"I mean, you've got to compare method with method, and ideal with ideal. I would say that since the war, our methods —ours and those of the opposition—have become much the same. I mean you can't be less ruthless than the opposition simply because your government's *policy* is benevolent, can you now?" He laughed quietly to himself. "That would *never* do," he said.

For God's sake, thought Leamas, it's like working for a bloody clergyman. What *is* he up to?

"That is why," Control continued, "I think we ought to try and get rid of Mundt. . . . Oh really," he said, turning irritably toward the door, "where is that damned coffee?"

Control crossed to the door, opened it and talked to some unseen girl in the outer room. As he returned he said: "I really think we *ought* to get rid of him if we can manage it."

"Why? We've got nothing left in East Germany, nothing at all. You just said so—Riemeck was the last. We've nothing left to protect."

Control sat down and looked at his hands for a while.

"That is not altogether true," he said finally; "but I don't think I need to bore you with the details."

Leamas shrugged.

"Tell me," Control continued, "are you tired of spying? Forgive me if I repeat the question. I mean that is a phenomenon we understand here, you know. Like aircraft designers . . . metal fatigue, I think the term is. Do say if you are."

Leamas remembered the flight home that morning and wondered.

"If you were," Control added, "we would have to find some other way of taking care of Mundt. What I have in mind is a little out of the ordinary."

The girl came in with the coffee. She put the tray on the desk and poured out two cups. Control waited till she had left the room.

"Such a *silly* girl," he said, almost to himself. "It seems extraordinary they can't find good ones any more. I do wish Ginnie wouldn't go on holiday at times like this." He stirred his coffee disconsolately for a while.

"We really must discredit Mundt," he said. "Tell me, do you drink a lot? Whisky and that kind of thing?"

Leamas had thought he was used to Control.

"I drink a bit. More than most, I suppose."

Control nodded understandingly. "What do you know about Mundt?"

"He's a killer. He was here a year or two back with the East German Steel Mission. We had an adviser here then: Maston."

"Quite so."

"Mundt was running an agent, the wife of an F.O. man. He killed her."

"He tried to kill George Smiley. And of course he shot the woman's husband. He is a very distasteful man. Ex Hitler-Youth and all that kind of thing. Not at all the intellectual kind of Communist. A practitioner of the cold war."

"Like us," Leamas observed drily.

Control didn't smile. "George Smiley knew the case well. He isn't with us any more, but I think you ought to ferret him out. He's doing things on seventeenth-century Germany.

He lives in Chelsea, just behind Sloane Square. Bywater Street, do you know it?"

"Yes."

"And Guillam was on the case as well. He's in Satellites Four, on the first floor. I'm afraid everything's changed since your day."

"Yes."

"Spend a day or two with them. They know what I have in mind. Then I wondered if you'd care to stay with me for the weekend. My wife," he added hastily, "is looking after her mother, I'm afraid. It will be just you and I."

"Thanks. I'd like to."

"We can talk about things in comfort then. It would be very nice. I think you might make a lot of money out of it. You can have whatever you make."

"Thanks."

"That is, of course, if you're *sure you want* to . . . no metal fatigue or anything?"

"If it's a question of killing Mundt, I'm game."

"Do you really feel that?" Control inquired politely. And then, having looked at Leamas thoughtfully for a moment, he observed, "Yes, I really think you do. But you mustn't feel you *have* to say it. I mean in our world we pass so quickly out of the register of hate or love—like certain sounds a dog can't hear. All that's left in the end is a kind of nausea; you never want to cause suffering again. Forgive me, but isn't that rather what you felt when Karl Riemeck was shot? Not hate for Mundt, nor love for Karl, but a sickening jolt like a blow on a numb body. . . . They tell me you walked all night—just walked through the streets of Berlin. Is that right?"

"It's right that I went for a walk."

"All night?"

"Yes."

"What happened to Elvira?"

"God knows. . . . I'd like to take a swing at Mundt," he said.

"Good . . . good. Incidentally, if you should meet any old friends in the meantime, I don't think there's any point in discussing this with them. In fact," Control added after a moment, "I should be rather short with them. Let them think we've treated you badly. It's as well to begin as one intends to continue, isn't it?"

✠ ✠ 3 ✠ Decline

It surprised no one very much when they put Leamas on the shelf. In the main, they said, Berlin had been a failure for years, and someone had to take the rap. Besides, he was old for operational work, where your reflexes often had to be as quick as those of a professional tennis player. Leamas had done good work in the war, everyone knew that. In Norway and Holland he had somehow remained demonstrably alive, and at the end of it they gave him a medal and let him go. Later, of course, they got him to come back. It was bad luck about his pension, decidedly bad luck. Accounts Section had let it out, in the person of Elsie. Elsie said in the canteen that poor Alec Leamas would only have £400 a year to live on because of his interrupted service. Elsie felt it was a rule they really ought to change; after all, Mr. Leamas had *done* the service, hadn't he? But there they were with Treasury on their backs, not a bit like the old days, and what could they do? Even in the bad days of Maston they'd managed things better.

Leamas, the new men were told, was the old school; blood, guts and cricket and High School French. In Leamas' case this happened to be unfair, since he was bilingual in German and English and his Dutch was admirable; he also disliked cricket. But it was true that he had no degree.

Leamas' contract had a few months to run, and they put him in Banking to do his time. Banking Section was different from Accounts; it dealt with overseas payments, financing agents and operations. Most of the jobs in Banking could have been done by an office boy were it not for the high degree of secrecy involved, and thus Banking was one of several sections of the Service which were regarded as laying-out places for officers shortly to be buried.

Leamas went to seed.

The process of going to seed is generally considered to be a protracted one, but in Leamas this was not the case. In the full view of his colleagues he was transformed from a man honorably put aside to a resentful, drunken wreck—and all within a few months. There is a kind of stupidity among drunks, particularly when they are sober, a kind of disconnection which the unobservant interpret as vagueness and which Leamas seemed to acquire with unnatural speed. He developed small dishonesties, borrowed insignificant sums from secretaries and neglected to return them, arrived late or left early under some mumbled pretext. At first his colleagues treated him with indulgence; perhaps his decline scared them in the same way as we are scared by cripples, beggars and invalids because we fear we could ourselves become them; but in the end his neglect, his brutal, unreasoning malice, isolated him.

Rather to people's surprise, Leamas didn't seem to mind being put on the shelf. His will seemed suddenly to have collapsed. The debutante secretaries, reluctant to believe that

Intelligence Services are peopled by ordinary mortals, were alarmed to notice that Leamas had become definitely seedy. He took less care of his appearance and less notice of his surroundings, he lunched in the canteen which was normally the preserve of junior staff, and it was obvious that he was drinking. He became a solitary, belonging to that tragic class of active men prematurely deprived of activity; swimmers barred from the water or actors banished from the stage.

Some said he had made a mistake in Berlin, and that was why his network had been rolled up; no one quite knew. All agreed that he had been treated with unusual harshness, even by a personnel department not famed for its philanthropy. They would point to him covertly as he went by, as men will point to an athlete of the past, and say: "That's Leamas. He made a mistake in Berlin. Pathetic the way he's let himself go."

And then one day he had vanished. He said good-bye to no one, not even, apparently, Control. In itself that was not surprising. The nature of the Service precluded elaborate farewells and the presentation of gold watches, but even by these standards Leamas' departure seemed abrupt. So far as could be judged, his departure occurred before the statutory termination of his contract. Elsie, of Accounts Section, offered one or two crumbs of information: Leamas had drawn the balance of his pay in cash, which if Elsie knew anything, meant he was having trouble with his bank. His severance pay was to be paid at the turn of the month, she couldn't say how much but it wasn't four figures, poor lamb. His National Insurance card had been sent on. Personnel had an address for him, Elsie added with a sniff, but of course they weren't revealing it, not Personnel.

Then there was the story about the money. It leaked out —no one, as usual, knew where from—that Leamas' sudden departure was connected with irregularities in the accounts of Banking Section. A largish sum was missing (not three figures but four, according to a lady with blue hair who worked in the telephone room) and they'd got it back, nearly all of it, and they'd stuck a lien on his pension. Others said they didn't believe it—if Alec had wanted to rob the till, they said, he'd know better ways of doing it than fiddling with H. Q. accounts. Not that he wasn't capable of it—he'd just have done it better. But those less impressed by Leamas' criminal potential pointed at his large consumption of alcohol, at the expense of maintaining a separate household, at the fatal disparity between pay at home and allowances abroad, and above all at the temptations put in the way of a man handling large sums of hot money when he knew that his days in the service were numbered. All agreed that if Alec had dipped his hands in the till he was finished for all time—the Resettlement people wouldn't look at him and Personnel would give him no reference—or one so icy cold that the most enthusiastic employer would shiver at the sight of it. Peculation was the one sin Personnel would never let you forget—and they never forgot it themselves. If it was true that Alec had robbed the Circus, he would take the wrath of Personnel with him to the grave—and Personnel would not so much as pay for the shroud.

For a week or two after his departure, a few people wondered what had become of him. But his former friends had already learned to keep clear of him. He had become a resentful bore, constantly attacking the Service and its administration, and what he called the "Cavalry boys" who, he said, managed its affairs as if it were a regimental club. He never missed an opportunity of railing against the Americans and their intelligence agencies. He seemed to hate them more than the Abteilung, to which he seldom, if ever, referred. He would hint that it was they who had compromised his network; this seemed to be an obsession with him, and it was poor reward for attempts to console him, it made him bad company, so that those who had known and even tacitly liked him, wrote him off. Leamas' departure caused only a ripple on the water; with other winds and the changing of the seasons it was soon forgotten.

His flat was small and squalid, done in brown paint with photographs of Clovelly. It looked directly onto the gray backs of three stone warehouses, the windows of which were drawn, for aesthetic reasons, in creosote. Above the warehouse there lived an Italian family, quarreling at night and beating carpets in the morning. Leamas had few possessions with which to brighten his rooms. He bought some shades to cover the light bulbs, and two pairs of sheets to replace the Hessian squares provided by the landlord. The rest Leamas tolerated: the flower pattern curtains, not lined or hemmed, the fraying brown carpets and the clumsy dark wood furniture, like something from a seamen's hostel. From a yellow crumbling geyser he obtained hot water for a shilling.

He needed a job. He had no money, none at all. So perhaps the stories of embezzlement were true. The offers of resettlement which the Service made had seemed to Leamas lukewarm and peculiarly unsuitable. He tried first to get a job in commerce. A firm of industrial adhesive manufacturers showed interest in his application for the post of assistant manager and personnel officer. Unconcerned by the inadequate reference with which the Service provided him, they demanded no qualifications and offered him six hundred a year. He stayed for a week, by which time the foul stench of decaying fish oil had permeated his clothes and hair, lingering in his nostrils like the smell of death. No amount of washing would remove it, so that in the end Leamas had his hair cut short to the scalp and threw away two of his best suits. He spent another week trying to sell encyclopedias to suburban housewives, but he was not a man that housewives liked or understood; they did not want Leamas, let alone his encyclopedias. Night after night he returned wearily to his flat, his ridiculous sample under his arm. At the end of a week he telephoned the company and told them he had sold nothing. Expressing no surprise, they reminded him of his obligation to return the sample if he discontinued acting on their behalf, and rang off. Leamas stalked out of the telephone booth in a fury leaving the sample behind him, went to a pub and got very drunk at a cost of twenty-five shillings, which he could not afford. They threw him out for shouting at a woman who tried to pick him up. They told him never to come back, but they'd forgotten all about it a week later. They were beginning to know Leamas there.

They were beginning to know him elsewhere too, the gray shambling figure from the Mansions. Not a wasted word did he speak, not a friend, neither man, woman nor beast, did he have. They guessed he was in trouble, run away from his wife like as not. He never knew the price of anything, never remembered it when he was told. He patted all his pockets whenever he looked for change, he never remembered to bring a basket, always buying shopping bags. They didn't like him in the Street, but they were almost sorry for him. They thought he was dirty, too, the way he didn't shave weekends and his shirts all grubby. A Mrs. McCaird from Sudbury Avenue cleaned for him for a week, but having never received a civil word from him withdrew her labor. She was an important source of information in the Street, where tradesmen told one another what they needed to know in case he asked for credit. Mrs. McCaird's advice was against credit. Leamas never had a letter, she said, and they agreed that that was serious. He'd no pictures and only a few books; she thought one of the books was dirty but couldn't be sure because it was in foreign writing. It was her opinion he had a bit to live on, and that that bit was running out. She knew he drew Benefit on Thursdays. Bayswater was warned, and needed no second warning. They heard from Mrs. McCaird that he drank like a fish: this was confirmed by the bartender. Bartenders and charwomen are not in the way of accommodating their clients with credit, but their information is treasured by those who are.

✠ ✠ 4 ✠ Liz

Finally he took the job in the library. The Labour Exchange put him on to it each Thursday morning as he drew his unemployment benefit, and he'd always turned it down.

"It's not really your cup of tea," Mr. Pitt said, "but the pay's fair and the work's easy for an educated man."

"What sort of library?" Leamas asked.

"It's the Bayswater Library for Psychic Research. It's an endowment. They've got thousands of volumes, all sorts, and they've been left a whole lot more. They want another helper."

He took his dole and the slip of paper. "They're an odd lot," Mr. Pitt added, "but then you're not a stayer anyway, are you? I think it's time you gave them a try, don't you?"

It was odd about Pitt. Leamas was certain he'd seen him before somewhere. At the Circus, during the war.

The library was like a church hall, and very cold. The black oil stoves at either end made it smell of paraffin. In the middle of the room was a cubicle like a witness box and inside it sat Miss Crail, the librarian.

It had never occurred to Leamas that he might have to work for a woman. No one at the Labour Exchange had said anything about that.

"I'm the new help," he said; "my name's Leamas."

Miss Crail looked up sharply from her card index, as if she had heard a rude word. "Help? What do you mean, help?"

"Assistant. From the Labour Exchange. Mr. Pitt." He pushed across the counter a form with his particulars entered in a sloping hand. She picked it up and studied it.

"You are Mr. Leamas." This was not a question, but the first stage of a laborious fact-finding investigation. "And you are from the Labour Exchange."

"No. I was sent by the Exchange. They told me you needed an assistant."

"I see." A wooden smile.

At that moment the telephone rang: she lifted the receiver and began arguing with somebody, fiercely. Leamas guessed they argued all the time; there were no preliminaries. Her voice just rose a key and she began arguing about some tickets for a concert. He listened for a minute or two and then drifted toward the bookshelves. He noticed a girl in one of the alcoves, standing on a ladder sorting large volumes.

"I'm the new man," he said, "my name's Leamas."

She came down from the ladder and shook his hand a little formally.

"I'm Liz Gold. How d'you do. Have you met Miss Crail?"

"Yes, but she's on the phone at the moment."

"Arguing with her mother I expect. What are you going to do?"

"I don't know. Work."

"We're marking at the moment; Miss Crail's started a new index."

She was a tall girl, ungainly, with a long waist and long legs. She wore flat, ballet type shoes to reduce her height. Her face, like her body, had large components which seemed to hesitate between plainness and beauty. Leamas guessed she was twenty-two or three, and Jewish.

"It's just a question of checking that all the books are in the shelves. This is the reference bit, you see. When you've checked, you pencil in the new reference and mark it off on the index."

"What happens then?"

"Only Miss Crail's allowed to ink in the reference. It's the rule."

"Whose rule?"

"Miss Crail's. Why don't you start on the archaeology?"

Leamas nodded and together they walked to the next alcove where a shoe box full of cards lay on the floor.

"Have you done this kind of thing before?" she asked.

"No." He stopped and picked up a handful of cards and shuffled through them. "Mr. Pitt sent me. From the Exchange." He put the cards back.

"Is Miss Crail the only person who can ink the cards, too?" Leamas inquired.

"Yes."

She left him there, and after a moment's hesitation he took out a book and looked at the fly-leaf. It was called *Archaeological Discoveries in Asia Minor. Volume Four.* They only seemed to have Volume Four.

It was one o'clock and Leamas was very hungry, so he walked over to where Liz Gold was sorting and said, "What happens about lunch?"

"Oh, I bring sandwiches." She looked a little embarrassed. "You can have some of mine if that would help. There's no café for miles."

Leamas shook his head.

"I'll go out, thanks. Got some shopping to do." She watched him push his way through the swing doors.

It was half past two when he came back. He smelled of whisky. He had one shopping bag full of vegetables and another containing groceries. He put them down in a corner of the alcove and wearily began again on the archaeology books. He'd been marking for about ten minutes when he became aware that Miss Crail was watching him.

"*Mister* Leamas."

He was halfway up the ladder, so he looked down over his shoulder and said, "Yes?"

"Do you know where these shopping bags come from?"

"They're mine."

"I see. They are yours." Leamas waited. "I regret," she continued at last, "that we do not allow it, bringing shopping into the library."

"Where else can I put it? There's nowhere else I *can* put it."

"Not in the library," she replied. Leamas ignored her, and returned his attention to the archaeology section.

"If you only took the normal lunch break," Miss Crail continued, "you would not have time to go shopping anyway. Neither of *us* does, Miss Gold or myself; *we* do not have time to shop."

"Why don't you take an extra half hour?" Leamas asked.

"You'd have time then. If you're pushed you can work another half hour in the evening. If you're pressed."

She stayed for some moments, just watching him and obviously thinking of something to say. Finally she announced: "I shall discuss it with Mr. Ironside," and went away.

At exactly half past five Miss Crail put on her coat and, with a pointed "Good night, Miss Gold," left. Leamas guessed she had been brooding on the shopping bags all afternoon. He went into the next alcove where Liz Gold was sitting on the bottom rung of her ladder reading what looked like a tract. When she saw Leamas she dropped it guiltily into her handbag and stood up.

"Who's Mr. Ironside?" Leamas asked.

"I don't think he exists," she replied. "He's her big gun when she's stuck for an answer. I asked her once who he was. She went all shifty and mysterious and said 'Never mind.' I don't think he exists."

"I'm not sure Miss Crail does," said Leamas, and Liz Gold smiled.

At six o'clock she locked up and gave the keys to the curator, a very old man with First World War shellshock who, said Liz, sat awake all night in case the Germans made a counterattack. It was bitterly cold outside.

"Got far to go?" asked Leamas.

"Twenty-minute walk. I always walk it. Have you?"

"Not far," said Leamas. "Good night."

He walked slowly back to the flat. He let himself in and turned the light switch. Nothing happened. He tried the light in the tiny kitchen and finally the electric fire that plugged in by his bed. On the doormat was a letter. He picked it up and took it out into the pale yellow light of the staircase. It was the electricity company, regretting that the area manager had no alternative but to cut off the electricity until the outstanding account of nine pounds, four shillings and eightpence had been settled.

He had become an enemy of Miss Crail, and enemies were what Miss Crail liked. Either she scowled at him or she ignored him, and when he came close, she began to tremble, looking to left and right, either for something with which to defend herself, or perhaps for a line of escape. Occasionally she would take immense umbrage, such as when he hung his mackintosh on *her* peg, and she stood in front of it shaking for fully five minutes, until Liz spotted her and called Leamas.

Leamas went over to her and said, "What's troubling you, Miss Crail?"

"Nothing," she replied in a breathy, clipped way, "nothing at all."

"Something wrong with my coat?"

"Nothing at all."

"Fine," he replied, and went back to his alcove. She quivered all that day, and conducted a telephone call in a stage whisper for half the morning.

"She's telling her mother," said Liz. "She always tells her mother. She tells her about me too."

Miss Crail developed such an intense hatred for Leamas that she found it impossible to communicate with him. On paydays he would come back from lunch and find an envelope on the third rung of his ladder with his name misspelled on the outside. The first time it happened he took the money over to her with the envelope and said, "It's L-E-A, Miss Crail, and only one s." Whereupon she was seized with a veritable palsy, rolling her eyes and fumbling erratically with her pencil until Leamas went away. She conspired into the telephone for hours after that.

About three weeks after Leamas began work at the library Liz asked him to supper. She pretended it was an idea that had come to her quite suddenly, at five o'clock that evening; she seemed to realize that if she were to ask him for tomorrow or the next day he would forget or just not come, so she asked him at five o'clock. Leamas seemed reluctant to accept, but in the end he did.

They walked to her flat through the rain and they might have been anywhere—Berlin, London, any town where paving stones turn to lakes of light in the evening rain, and the traffic shuffles despondently through wet streets.

It was the first of many meals which Leamas had at her flat. He came when she asked him, and she asked him often. He never spoke much. When she discovered he would come, she took to laying the table in the morning before leaving for the library. She even prepared the vegetables beforehand and had the candles on the table, for she loved candlelight. She always knew that there was something deeply wrong with Leamas, and that one day, for some reason she could not understand, he might break and she would never see him again.

She tried to tell him she knew; she said to him one evening: "You must go when you want. I'll never follow you, Alec."

His brown eyes rested on her for a moment: "I'll tell you when," he replied.

Her flat was a bed-sitting-room and a kitchen. In the sitting room were two armchairs, a sofa-bed, and a bookcase full of paperback books, mainly classics which she had never read.

After supper she would talk to him, and he would lie on the sofa, smoking. She never knew how much he heard, she didn't care. She would kneel by the sofa holding his hand against her cheek, talking.

Then one evening she said to him, "Alec, what do you believe in? Don't laugh—tell me." She waited and at last he said:

"I believe an eleven bus will take me to Hammersmith. I don't believe it's driven by Father Christmas."

She seemed to consider this and at last she asked again: "But what do you believe in?"

Leamas shrugged.

"You must believe in something," she persisted: "something like God—I know you do, Alec; you've got that look sometimes, as if you'd got something special to do, like a priest. Alec, don't smile, it's true."

He shook his head.

"Sorry, Liz, you've got it wrong. I don't like Americans and public schools. I don't like military parades and people who play soldiers." Without smiling he added, "And I don't like conversations about Life."

"But Alec, you might as well say—"

"I should have added," Leamas interrupted, "that I don't like people who tell me what I ought to think." She knew he was getting angry but she couldn't stop herself any more.

"That's because you don't *want* to think, you don't dare! There's some poison in your mind, some hate. You're a fanatic, Alec, I know you are, but I don't know what about. You're a fanatic who doesn't want to convert people, and that's a dangerous thing. You're like a man who's . . . sworn vengeance or something."

The brown eyes rested on her. When he spoke she was frightened by the menace in his voice.

"If I were you," he said roughly, "I'd mind my own business."

And then he smiled, a roguish Irish smile. He hadn't smiled like that before and Liz knew he was putting on the charm.

"What does Liz believe in?" he asked, and she replied:

"I can't be had that easy, Alec."

Later that night they talked about it again. Leamas brought it up—he asked her whether she was religious.

"You've got me wrong," she said, "all wrong. I don't believe in God."

"Then what do you believe in?"

"History."

He looked at her in astonishment for a moment, then laughed.

"Oh Liz . . . oh *no!* You're not a bloody Communist?"

She nodded, blushing like a small girl at his laughter, angry and relieved that he didn't care.

She made him stay that night and they became lovers. He left at five in the morning. She couldn't understand it; she was so proud and he seemed ashamed.

He left her flat and turned down the empty street toward the park. It was foggy. Some way down the road—not far, twenty yards, perhaps a bit more—stood the figure of a man in a raincoat, short and rather plump. He was leaning against the railings of the .park, silhouetted in the shifting mist. As Leamas approached, the mist seemed to thicken, closing in around the figure at the railings, and when it parted the man was gone.

⚔ ⚔ 5 ⚔ Credit

Then one day about a week later, he didn't come to the library. Miss Crail was delighted; by half-past eleven she had told her mother, and on returning from lunch she stood in front of the archaeology shelves where he had been working since he came. She stared with theatrical concentration at the rows of books, and Liz knew she was pretending to work out whether Leamas had stolen anything.

Liz entirely ignored her for the rest of that day, failed to reply when she addressed her, and worked with assiduous application. When the evening came she walked home and cried herself to sleep.

The next morning she arrived early at the library. She somehow felt that the sooner she got there, the sooner Leamas might come; but as the morning dragged on her hopes faded, and she knew he would never come. She had forgotten to make sandwiches for herself that day so she decided to take a bus to the Bayswater Road and go to the

A.B.C. Café. She felt sick and empty, but not hungry. Should she go and find him? She had promised never to follow him, but he had promised to tell her; should she go and find him?

She hailed a taxi and gave his address.

She made her way up the dingy staircase and pressed the bell of his door. The bell seemed to be broken; she heard nothing. There were three bottles of milk on the mat and a letter from the electricity company. She hesitated a moment, then banged on the door, and she heard the faint groan of a man. She rushed downstairs to the flat below, hammered and rang at the door. There was no reply so she ran down another flight and found herself in the back room of a grocer's shop. An old woman sat in a corner, rocking back and forth in her chair.

"The top flat," Liz almost shouted, "somebody's very ill. Who's got a key?"

The old woman looked at her for a moment, then called toward the front room, where the shop was.

"Arthur, come in here, Arthur, there's a girl here!"

A man in brown overalls and a gray trilby hat looked round the door and said, "Girl?"

"There's someone seriously ill in the top flat," said Liz. "He can't get to the front door to open it. Have you a key?"

"No," replied the grocer, "but I've got a hammer," and they hurried up the stairs together, the grocer, still in his trilby, carrying a heavy screwdriver and a hammer. He knocked on the door sharply, and they waited breathless for an answer. There was none.

"I heard a groan before, I promise I did," Liz whispered.

"Will you pay for this door if I bust it?"

"Yes."

The hammer made a terrible noise. With three blows he had wrenched out a piece of the frame and the lock came with it. Liz went in first and the grocer followed. It was bitterly cold in the room and dark, but on the bed in the corner they could make out the figure of a man.

Oh God, thought Liz, if he's dead I don't think I can touch him. But she went to him and he was alive. Drawing the curtains, she knelt beside the bed.

"I'll call you if I need you, thank you," she said without looking back, and the grocer nodded and went downstairs.

"Alec, what is it, what's making you ill? What is it, Alec?"

Leamas moved his head on the pillow. His sunken eyes were closed. The dark beard stood out against the pallor of his face.

"Alec, you must tell me, please, Alec." She was holding one of his hands in hers. The tears were running down her cheeks. Desperately she wondered what to do; then, getting up, she ran to the tiny kitchen and put on a kettle. She wasn't quite clear what she would make, but it comforted her to do something. Leaving the kettle on the gas she picked up her handbag, took Leamas' key from the bedside table and ran downstairs, down the four flights into the street, and crossed the road to Mr. Sleaman, the chemist. She bought some calf's-foot jelly, some breast of chicken, some essence of beef and a bottle of Aspirin. She got to the door, then went back and bought a packet of rusks. Altogether it cost her sixteen shillings, which left four shillings in her handbag and eleven pounds in her postoffice savings bank book, but she couldn't draw any of that till tomorrow. By the time she returned to his flat the kettle was just boiling.

She made the beef tea like her mother used to in a glass

with a teaspoon in to stop its cracking, and all the time she glanced toward him as if she were afraid he was dead.

She had to prop him up to make him drink the tea. He had only one pillow and there were no cushions in the room, so taking his overcoat down from the back of the door she made a bundle of it and arranged it behind the pillow. It frightened her to touch him; he was so drenched in sweat that his short gray hair was damp and slippery. Putting the cup beside the bed, she held his head with one hand and fed him the tea with the other. After he had taken a few spoonfuls, she crushed two Aspirin and gave them to him in the spoon. She talked to him as if he were a child, sitting on the edge of the bed looking at him, sometimes letting her fingers run over his head and face, whispering his name over and over again: "Alec, Alec."

Gradually his breathing became more regular, his body more relaxed, as he drifted from the taut pain of fever to the calm of sleep; Liz, watching him, sensed that the worst was over. Suddenly she realized it was almost dark.

Then she felt ashamed because she knew she should have cleaned and tidied. Jumping up, she fetched the carpet sweeper and a duster from the kitchen and set to work with feverish energy. She found a clean teacloth and spread it neatly on the bedside table and she washed up the odd cups and saucers which lay around the kitchen. When everything was done she looked at her watch and it was half-past eight. She put the kettle on and went back to the bed. Leamas was looking at her.

"Alec, don't be cross, please don't," she said. "I'll go, I promise I will, but let me make you a proper meal. You're ill, you can't go on like this, you're—Oh, Alec," and she broke down and wept, holding both hands over her face, the tears running between her fingers like the tears of a child. He let her cry, watching her with his brown eyes, his hands holding the sheet.

She helped him wash and shave and she found some clean bedclothes. She gave him some calf's-foot jelly, and some breast of chicken from the jar she'd bought at Mr. Sleaman's. Sitting on the bed she watched him eat, and she thought she had never been so happy before.

Soon he fell asleep, and she drew the blanket over his shoulders and went to the window. Parting the threadbare curtains, she raised the sash and looked out. The two windows in the courtyard above the warehouse were lit. In one she could see the flickering blue shadow of a television screen, the figures before it held motionless in its spell; in the other a woman, quite young, was arranging curlers in her hair. Liz wanted to weep at the crabbed delusion of their dreams.

She fell asleep in the armchair and did not wake until it was nearly light, feeling stiff and cold. She went to the bed: Leamas stirred as she looked at him and she touched his lips with the tip of her finger. He did not open his eyes but gently took her arm and drew her down onto the bed, and suddenly she wanted him terribly, and nothing mattered, and she kissed him again and again and when she looked at him he seemed to be smiling.

She came every day for six days. He never spoke to her much and once, when she asked him if he loved her, he said he didn't believe in fairy tales. She would lie on the bed, her head against his chest, and sometimes he would put his thick fingers in her hair, holding it quite tight, and Liz laughed and said it hurt. On Friday evening she found him dressed but not shaved, and she wondered why he hadn't shaved. For some imperceptible reason she was alarmed. Little things were missing from the room—his clock and the cheap portable radio that had been on the table. She wanted to ask and did not dare. She had bought some eggs and ham and she cooked them for their supper while Leamas sat on the bed and smoked one cigarette after another. When supper was ready he went to the kitchen and came back with a bottle of red wine.

He hardly spoke at supper, and she watched him, her fear growing until she could bear it no more and she cried out suddenly, "Alec . . . oh Alec . . . what is it? Is it good-bye?"

He got up from the table, took her hands and kissed her in a way he'd never done before, and spoke to her softly for a long time, told her things she only dimly understood, only half heard because all the time she knew it was the end and nothing mattered any more.

"Good-bye, Liz," he said. "Good-bye," and then: "Don't follow me. Not again."

Liz nodded and muttered, "Like we said." She was thankful for the biting cold of the street and for the dark which hid her tears.

It was the next morning, a Saturday, that Leamas asked at the grocer's for credit. He did it without much artistry, in a way not calculated to ensure him success. He ordered half a dozen items—they didn't come to more than a pound—and when they had been wrapped and put into the shopping bag he said, "You'd better send me that account."

The grocer smiled a difficult smile and said, "I'm afraid I can't do that." The "sir" was definitely missing.

"Why the hell not?" asked Leamas, and the queue behind him stirred uneasily.

"Don't know you," replied the grocer.

"Don't be bloody silly," said Leamas, "I've been coming here for four months."

The grocer colored. "We always ask for a banker's reference before giving credit," he said, and Leamas lost his temper.

"Don't talk bloody cock!" he shouted. "Half your customers have never seen the inside of a bank and never bloody well will." This was heresy beyond bearing, since it was true.

"I don't know you," the grocer repeated thickly, "and I don't like you. Now get out of my shop." And he tried to recover the parcel which unfortunately Leamas was already holding.

Opinions later differed as to what happened next. Some said the grocer, in trying to recover the bag, pushed Leamas; others say he did not. Whether he did or not, Leamas hit him, most people think twice, without disengaging his right hand, which still held the shopping bag. He seemed to deliver the blow not with his fist but with the side of his left hand, and then, as part of the same phenomenally rapid movement, with the left elbow; and the grocer fell straight over and lay as still as a rock. It was said in court later, and not contested by the defense, that the grocer had two injuries—a fractured cheekbone from the first blow and a dislocated jaw from the second. The coverage in the daily press was adequate, but not overelaborate.

⌖ ⌖ 6 ⌖ Contact

At night he lay on his bunk listening to the sounds of the prisoners. There was a boy who sobbed and an old lag who sang "On Ilkley Moor bar t'at," beating out the time on his food tin. There was a warder who shouted, "Shut up, George, you miserable sod," after each verse, but no one took any notice. There was an Irishman who sang songs about the IRA, though the others said he was in for rape.

Leamas took as much exercise as he could during the day in the hope that he would sleep at night; but it was no good. At night you knew you were in prison: at night there was nothing, no trick of vision or self-delusion which saved you from the nauseating enclosure of the cell. You could not keep out the taste of prison, the smell of prison uniform, the stench of prison sanitation heavily disinfected, the noises of captive men. It was then, at night, that the indignity of captivity became urgently insufferable, it was then that Leamas longed to walk in the friendly sunshine of a London park. It was then that he hated the grotesque steel cage that held him, had to force back the urge to fall upon the bars with his bare fists, to split the skulls of his guards and burst into the free, free space of London. Sometimes he thought of Liz. He would direct his mind toward her briefly like the shutter of a camera, recall for a moment the soft-hard touch of her long body, then put her from his memory. Leamas was not a man accustomed to living on dreams.

He was contemptuous of his cellmates, and they hated him. They hated him because he succeeded in being what each in his heart longed to be: a mystery. He preserved from collectivization some discernible part of his personality; he could not be drawn at moments of sentiment to talk of his girl, his family or his children. They knew nothing of Leamas; they waited, but he did not come to them. New prisoners are largely of two kinds—there are those who for shame, fear or shock wait in fascinated horror to be initiated into the lore of prison life, and there are those who trade on their wretched novelty in order to endear themselves to the community. Leamas did neither of these things. He seemed pleased to despise them all, and they hated him because, like the world outside, he did not need them.

After about ten days they had had enough. The great had had no homage, the small had had no comfort, so they crowded him in the dinner queue. Crowding is a prison ritual akin to the eighteenth-century practice of jostling. It has the virtue of an apparent accident, in which the prisoner's mess tin is upturned and its contents spilled on his uniform. Leamas was barged from one side, while from the other an obliging hand descended on his forearm, and the thing was done. Leamas said nothing, looked thoughtfully at the two men on either side of him, and accepted in silence the filthy rebuke of a warder who knew quite well what had happened.

Four days later, while working with a hoe on the prison flower bed, he seemed to stumble. He was holding the hoe with both hands across his body, the end of the handle protruding about six inches from his right fist. As he strove to recover his balance the prisoner to his right doubled up with a grunt of agony, his arms across his stomach. There was no more crowding after that.

Perhaps the strangest thing of all about prison was the brown paper parcel when he left. In a ridiculous way it reminded him of the marriage service—with this ring I thee wed, with this paper parcel I return thee to society. They handed it to him and made him sign for it, and it contained all he had in the world. There was nothing else. Leamas felt it the most dehumanizing moment of the three months, and he determined to throw the parcel away as soon as he got outside.

He seemed a quiet prisoner. There had been no complaints against him. The Governor, who was vaguely interested in his case, secretly put the whole thing down to the Irish blood he swore he could detect in Leamas.

"What are you going to do," he asked, "when you leave here?" Leamas replied, without a ghost of a smile, that he thought he would make a new start, and the Governor said that was an excellent thing to do.

"What about your family?" he asked. "Couldn't you make it up with your wife?"

"I'll try," Leamas had replied indifferently; "but she's remarried."

The probation officer wanted Leamas to become a male nurse at a mental home in Buckinghamshire and Leamas agreed to apply. He even took down the address and noted the train times from Marylebone.

"The rail's electrified as far as Great Missenden, now," the probation officer added, and Leamas said that would be a help. So they gave him the parcel and he left. He took a bus to Marble Arch and walked. He had a bit of money in his pocket and he intended to give himself a decent meal. He thought he would walk through Hyde Park to Piccadilly, then through Green Park and St. James's Park to Parliament Square, then wander down Whitehall to the Strand where he could go to the big café near Charing Cross Station and get a reasonable steak for six shillings.

London was beautiful that day. Spring was late and the parks were filled with crocuses and daffodils. A cool, cleaning wind was blowing from the south; he could have walked all day. But he still had the parcel and he had to get rid of it. The litter baskets were too small; he'd look absurd trying to push his parcel into one of those. He supposed there were one or two things he ought to take out, his wretched pieces of paper—insurance card, driving license and his E.93 (whatever that was) in a buff OHMS envelope—but suddenly he couldn't be bothered. He sat down on a bench and put the parcel beside him, not too close, and moved a little away from it. After a couple of minutes he walked back toward the footpath, leaving the parcel where it lay. He had just reached the footpath when he heard a shout; he turned, a little sharply perhaps, and saw a man in an army mackintosh beckoning to him, holding the brown paper parcel in the other hand.

Leamas had his hands in his pockets and he left them there, and stood, looking back over his shoulder at the man in the mackintosh. The man hesitated, evidently expecting Leamas to come to him or give some sign of interest, but Leamas gave none. Instead, he shrugged and continued along the footpath. He heard another shout and ignored it, and he knew the man was coming after him. He heard the footsteps on the gravel, half running, approaching rapidly, and then a voice, a little breathless, a little aggravated:

"Here you—I say!" and then he had drawn level, so that Leamas stopped, turned and looked at him.

"Yes?"

"This is your parcel, isn't it? You left it on the seat. Why didn't you stop when I called you?"

Tall, with rather curly brown hair; orange tie and pale green shirt; a little bit petulant, a little bit of a pansy, thought Leamas. Could be a schoolmaster, ex-London School of Economics and runs a suburban drama club. Weak-eyed.

"You can put it back," said Leamas. "I don't want it."

The man colored. "You can't just leave it there," he said, "it's litter."

"I bloody well can," Leamas replied. "Somebody will find a use for it." He was going to move on, but the stranger was still standing in front of him, holding the parcel in both arms as if it were a baby. "Get out of the light," said Leamas. "Do you mind?"

"Look here," said the stranger, and his voice had risen a key, "I was trying to do you a favor; why do you have to be so damned rude?"

"If you're so anxious to do me a favor," Leamas replied, "why have you been following me for the last half hour?"

He's pretty good, thought Leamas. He hasn't flinched but he must be shaken rigid.

"I thought you were somebody I once knew in Berlin, if you must know."

"So you followed me for half an hour?"

Leamas' voice was heavy with sarcasm, his brown eyes never left the other's face.

"Nothing like half an hour. I caught sight of you in Marble Arch and I thought you were Alec Leamas, a man I borrowed some money from. I used to be in the BBC in Berlin and there was this man I borrowed some money from. I've had a bad conscience about it ever since and that's why I followed you. I wanted to be sure."

Leamas went on looking at him, not speaking, and thought he wasn't all that good but he was good enough. His story was scarcely plausible—that didn't matter. The point was that he'd produced a new one and stuck to it after Leamas had wrecked what promised to be a classic approach.

"I'm Leamas," he said at last. "Who the hell are you?"

He said his name was Ashe, with an "ᴇ" he added quickly, and Leamas knew he was lying. He pretended not to be quite sure that Leamas really was Leamas, so over lunch they opened the parcel and looked at the National Insurance card like, thought Leamas, a couple of sissies looking at a dirty postcard. Ashe ordered lunch with just a fraction too little regard for expense, and they drank some Frankenwein to remind them of the old days. Leamas began by insisting he couldn't remember Ashe, and Ashe said he was surprised. He said it in the sort of tone that suggested he was hurt. They met at a party, he said, which Derek Williams gave in his flat off the Ku-damm (he got that right), and all the press boys had been there; surely Alec remembered that? No, Leamas did not. Well surely he remembered Derek Williams from the *Observer*, that *nice* man who gave such lovely pizza parties? Leamas had a lousy memory for names, after all they were talking about '54; a lot of water had flown under the bridge since then. . . . Ashe remembered (his Christian name was William, by-the-bye, most people called him Bill), Ashe re-

membered *vividly*. They'd been drinking stingers, brandy
and crème de menthe, and were all rather tiddly, and Derek
had provided some really gorgeous girls, half the cabaret
from the Malkasten, *surely* Alec remembered now? Leamas
thought it was probably coming back to him, if Bill would
go on a bit.

Bill did go on, ad-lib no doubt, but he did it well, playing
up the sex side a little, how they'd finished up in a night club
with three of these girls; Alec, a chap from the political adviser's office and Bill, and Bill had been so embarrassed because he hadn't any money on him and Alec had paid, and
Bill had wanted to take a girl home and Alec had lent him
another tenner—

"Christ," said Leamas, "I remember now, of course I do."

"I *knew* you would," said Ashe happily, nodding at Leamas over his glass. "Look, do let's have the other half, this is
such fun."

Ashe was typical of that strata of mankind which conducts
its human relationships according to a principle of challenge
and response. Where there was softness, he would advance;
where he found resistance, retreat. Having himself no particular opinions or tastes, he relied upon whatever conformed
with those of his companion. He was as ready to drink tea at
Fortnum's as beer at the Prospect of Whitby; he would listen
to military music in St. James's Park or jazz in a Compton
Street cellar; his voice would tremble with sympathy when
he spoke of Sharpeville, or with indignation at the growth of
Britain's colored population. To Leamas this observably
passive role was repellent; it brought out the bully in him, so
that he would lead the other gently into a position where he

was committed, and then himself withdraw, so that Ashe was constantly scampering back from some cul-de-sac into which Leamas had enticed him. There were moments that afternoon when Leamas was so brazenly perverse that Ashe would have been justified in terminating their conversation —especially since he was paying; but he did not. The little sad man with spectacles who sat alone at the neighboring table, deep in a book on the manufacture of ball bearings, might have deduced, had he been listening, that Leamas was indulging a sadistic nature—or perhaps (if he had been a man of particular subtlety) that Leamas was proving to his own satisfaction that only a man with a strong ulterior motive would put up with that kind of treatment.

It was nearly four o'clock before they ordered the bill, and Leamas tried to insist on paying his half. Ashe wouldn't hear of it, paid the bill and took out his checkbook in order to settle his debt to Leamas.

"Twenty of the best," he said, and filled in the date on the check form.

Then he looked up at Leamas, all wide-eyed and accommodating. "I say, a check is all right with you, isn't it?"

Coloring a little, Leamas replied, "I haven't got a bank at the moment—only just back from abroad, something I've got to fix up. Better give me a check and I'll cash it at your bank."

"My dear chap, I wouldn't *dream* of it! You'd have to go to Rotherhithe to cash this one!" Leamas shrugged and Ashe laughed, and they agreed to meet at the same place on the following day, at one o'clock, when Ashe would have the money in cash.

Ashe took a cab at the corner of Compton Street, and Leamas waved at it until it was out of sight. When it was gone, he looked at his watch. It was four o'clock. He guessed he was still being followed, so he walked down to Fleet Street and had a cup of coffee in the Black and White. He looked at bookshops, read the evening papers displayed in the show windows of newspaper offices, and then quite suddenly, as if the thought had occurred to him at the last minute, he jumped on a bus. The bus went to Ludgate Hill, where it was held up in a traffic jam near a tube station; he dismounted and caught a tube. He bought a sixpenny ticket, stood in the end car and got off at the next station. He caught another train to Euston, trekked back to Charing Cross. It was nine o'clock when he reached the station and it had turned rather cold. There was a van waiting in the forecourt; the driver was fast asleep.

Leamas glanced at the number, went over and called through the window, "Are you from Clements?"

The driver woke up with a start and asked, "Mr. Thomas?"

"No," replied Leamas. "Thomas couldn't come. I'm Amies from Hounslow."

"Hop in, Mr. Amies," the driver replied, and opened the door. They drove West, toward the King's Road. The driver knew the way.

Control opened the door.

"George Smiley's out," he said. "I've borrowed his house. Come in." Not until Leamas was inside and the front door closed, did Control put on the hall light.

"I was followed till lunchtime," Leamas said. They went into the little drawing room. There were books everywhere. It was a pretty room; tall, with eighteenth-century moldings, long windows and a good fireplace. "They picked me up this morning. A man called Ashe." He lit a cigarette. "A pansy. We're meeting again tomorrow."

Control listened carefully to Leamas' story, stage by stage, from the day he hit Ford the grocer to his encounter that morning with Ashe.

"How did you find prison?" Control inquired. He might have been asking whether Leamas had enjoyed his holiday. "I am sorry we couldn't improve conditions for you, provide little extra comforts, but that would never have done."

"Of course not."

"One must be consistent. At every turn one must be consistent. Besides, it would be wrong to break the spell. I understand you were ill. I am sorry. What was the trouble?"

"Just fever."

"How long were you in bed?"

"About ten days."

"How very distressing; and nobody to look after you, of course."

There was a very long silence.

"You know she's in the Party, don't you?" Control asked quietly.

"Yes," Leamas replied. Another silence. "I don't want her brought into this."

"Why should she be?" Control asked sharply and for a moment, just for a moment, Leamas thought he had penetrated the veneer of academic detachment. "Who suggested she should be?"

"No one," Leamas replied. "I'm just making the point. I know how these things go—all offensive operations. They have by-products, take sudden turns in unexpected directions. You think you've caught one fish and you find you've caught another. I want her kept clear of it."

"Oh quite, quite."

"Who's that man in the Labour Exchange—Pitt? Wasn't he in the Circus during the war?"

"I know no one of that name. Pitt, did you say?"

"Yes."

"No, the name means nothing to me. In the Labour Exchange?"

"Oh, for God's sake," Leamas muttered audibly.

"I'm sorry," said Control, getting up, "I'm neglecting my duties as deputy host. Would you care for a drink?"

"No. I want to get away tonight, Control. Go down to the country and get some exercise. Is the House open?"

"I've arranged a car," he said. "What time do you see Ashe tomorrow—one o'clock?"

"Yes."

"I'll ring Haldane and tell him you want some squash. You'd better see a doctor, too. About that fever."

"I don't need a doctor."

"Just as you like."

Control gave himself a whisky and began looking idly at the books in Smiley's shelf.

"Why isn't Smiley here?" Leamas asked.

"He doesn't like the operation," Control replied indifferently. "He finds it distasteful. He sees the necessity but he wants no part in it. His fever," Control added with a whimsical smile, "is recurrent."

"He didn't exactly receive me with open arms."

"Quite. He wants no part in it. But he told you about Mundt; gave you the background?"

"Yes."

"Mundt is a very *hard* man," Control reflected. "We should never forget that. And a good intelligence officer."

"Does Smiley know the reason for the operation? The special interest?"

Control nodded and took a sip of whisky.

"And he still doesn't like it?"

"It isn't a question of moralities. He is like the surgeon who has grown tired of blood. He is content that others should operate."

"Tell me," Leamas continued, "how are you so certain this will get us where we want? How do you know the East Germans are on to it—not the Czechs or the Russians?"

"Rest assured," Control said a little pompously, "that that has been taken care of."

As they got to the door, Control put his hand lightly on Leamas' shoulder.

"This is your last job," he said. "Then you can come in from the cold. About that girl—do you want anything done about her, money or anything?"

"When it's over. I'll take care of it myself then."

"Quite. It would be very insecure to do anything now."

"I just want her left alone," Leamas repeated with emphasis. "I just don't want her to be messed about. I don't want her to have a file or anything. I want her forgotten."

He nodded to Control and slipped out into the night air. Into the cold.

✠ ✠ 7 ✠ Kiever

On the following day, Leamas arrived twenty minutes late for his lunch with Ashe, and smelled of whisky. Ashe's pleasure on catching sight of Leamas was, however, undiminished. He claimed that he had himself only that moment arrived, he'd been a little late getting to the bank. He handed Leamas an envelope.

"Singles," said Ashe. "I hope that's all right?"

"Thanks," Leamas replied, "let's have a drink." He hadn't shaved and his collar was filthy. He called the waiter and ordered drinks, a large whisky for himself and a pink gin for Ashe. When the drinks came, Leamas' hand trembled as he poured the soda into the glass, almost slopping it over the side.

They lunched well, with a lot to drink, and Ashe did most of the work. As Leamas had expected he first talked about himself, an old trick but not a bad one.

"To be quite frank, I've got on to rather a good thing recently," said Ashe; "free-lancing English features for the foreign press. After Berlin I made rather a mess of things at first—the Corporation wouldn't renew the contract and I took a job running a dreary toffee-shop weekly about hobbies for the over-sixties. Can you *imagine* anything more frightful? That went under in the first printing strike—I can't tell you how relieved I was. Then I went to live with my mama in Cheltenham for a time—she runs an antique shop, does very nicely thank you, as a matter of fact. Then I got a letter from an old friend, Sam Kiever his name is actually, who was starting up a new agency for small features on English life specially slanted for foreign papers. You know the sort of thing—six hundred words on Morris dancing. Sam had a new gimmick, though; he sold the stuff already translated and do you know, it makes a hell of a difference. One always imagines anyone can pay a translator or do it themselves, but if you're looking for a half column in-fill for your foreign features you don't *want* to waste time and money on translation. Sam's gambit was to get in touch with the editors direct—he traipsed round Europe like a gypsy, poor thing, but it's paid hands *down*."

Ashe paused, waiting for Leamas to accept the invitation to speak about himself, but Leamas ignored it. He just nodded dully and said, "Bloody good." Ashe had wanted to order wine, but Leamas said he'd stick to whisky, and by the time the coffee came he'd had four large ones. He seemed to be in bad shape; he had the drunkard's habit of ducking his mouth toward the rim of his glass just before he drank, as if his hand might fail him and the drink escape.

Ashe fell silent for a moment.

"You don't know Sam, do you?" he asked.

"Sam?"

A note of irritation entered Ashe's voice.

"Sam Kiever, my boss. The chap I was telling you about."

"Was he in Berlin too?"

"No. He knows Germany well, but he's never lived in Berlin. He did a bit of deviling in Bonn, free-lance stuff. You might have met him. He's a dear."

"Don't think so." A pause.

"What do you do these days, old chap?" asked Ashe.

Leamas shrugged. "I'm on the shelf," he replied, and grinned a little stupidly. "Out of the bag and on the shelf."

"I forget what you were doing in Berlin. Weren't you one of the mysterious cold warriors?"

My God, thought Leamas, you're stepping things up a bit. Leamas hesitated, then colored and said savagely, "Office boy for the bloody Yanks, like the rest of us."

"You know," said Ashe, as if he had been turning the idea over for some time, "you ought to meet Sam. You'd like him," and then, all of a bother, "I say, Alec—I don't even know where to get hold of you!"

"You can't," Leamas replied listlessly.

"I don't get you, old chap. Where are you staying?"

"Around the place. Roughing it a bit. I haven't got a job. Bastards wouldn't give me a proper pension."

Ashe looked horrified.

"But Alec, that's awful, why didn't you *tell* me? Look, why not come and stay at my place? It's only tiny but there's room for one more if you don't mind a camp bed. You can't just live in the trees, my dear chap!"

"I'm all right for a bit," Leamas replied, tapping at the pocket which contained the envelope. "I'm going to get a job." He nodded with determination. "Get one in a week or so. Then I'll be all right."

"What sort of job?"

"Oh, I don't know. Anything."

"But you can't just throw yourself away, Alec! You speak German like a native, I remember you do. There must be all sorts of things you can do!"

"I've done all sorts of things. Selling encyclopedias for some bloody American firm, sorting books in a psychic library, punching work tickets in a stinking glue factory. What the hell *can* I do?" He wasn't looking at Ashe but at the table before him, his agitated lips moving quickly. Ashe responded to his animation, leaning forward across the table, speaking with emphasis, almost triumph.

"But Alec, you need *contacts*, don't you see? I know what it's like, I've been on the breadline myself. That's when you need to *know* people. I don't know what you were doing in Berlin, I don't want to know, but it wasn't the sort of job where you could meet people who matter, was it? If I hadn't met Sam at Poznan five years ago I'd *still* be on the breadline. Look, Alec, come and stay with me for a week or so. We'll ask Sam around and perhaps one or two of the old press boys from Berlin if any of them are in town."

"But I can't write," said Leamas. "I couldn't write a bloody thing."

Ashe had his hand on Leamas' arm. "Now don't fuss," he said soothingly. "Let's just take things one at a time. Where are your bits and pieces?"

"My what?"

"Your things: clothes, baggage and what not?"

"I haven't got any. I've sold what I had—except the parcel."

"What parcel?"

"The brown paper parcel you picked up in the park. The one I was trying to throw away."

Ashe had a flat in Dolphin Square. It was just what Leamas had expected—small and anonymous with a few hastily assembled curios from Germany: beer mugs, a peasant's pipe and a few pieces of second-rate Nymphenburg.

"I spend the weekends with my mother in Cheltenham," he said. "I just use this place midweek. It's pretty handy," he added deprecatingly. They fixed the camp bed up in the tiny drawing room. It was about four-thirty.

"How long have you been here?" asked Leamas.

"Oh—about a year or more."

"Find it easily?"

"They come and go, you know, these flats. You put your name down and one day they ring you up and tell you you've made it."

Ashe made tea and they drank it, Leamas sullen, like a man not used to comfort. Even Ashe seemed a little subdued. After tea Ashe said, "I'll go out and do a spot of shopping before the shops close, then we'll decide what to do about everything. I might give Sam a tinkle later this evening—I think the sooner you two get together the better. Why don't you get some sleep—you look all in."

Leamas nodded. "It's bloody good of you"—he made an awkward gesture with his hand—"all this." Ashe gave him a pat on the shoulder, picked up his army mackintosh and left.

As soon as Leamas reckoned Ashe was safely out of the building he left the front door of the flat slightly ajar and made his way downstairs to the center hall, where there were two telephone booths. He dialed a Maida Vale number and asked for Mr. Thomas' secretary. Immediately a girl's voice said, "Mr. Thomas' secretary speaking."

"I'm ringing on behalf of Mr. Sam Kiever," Leamas said.

"He has accepted the invitation and hopes to contact Mr. Thomas personally this evening."

"I'll pass that on to Mr. Thomas. Does he know where to get in touch with you?"

"Dolphin Square," Leamas replied, and gave the address. "Good-bye."

After making some inquiries at the reception desk, he returned to Ashe's flat and sat on the camp bed looking at his clasped hands. After a while he lay down. He decided to accept Ashe's advice and get some rest. As he closed his eyes he remembered Liz lying beside him in the flat in Bayswater, and he wondered vaguely what had become of her.

He was wakened by Ashe, accompanied by a small, rather plump man with long, graying hair swept back and a double-breasted suit. He spoke with a slight central European accent; German perhaps, it was hard to tell. He said his name was Kiever—Sam Kiever.

They had a gin and tonic, Ashe doing most of the talking. It was just like old times, he said, in Berlin: the boys together and the night their oyster. Kiever said he didn't want to be too late; he had to work tomorrow. They agreed to eat at a Chinese restaurant that Ashe knew of—it was opposite Limehouse police station and you brought your own wine. Oddly enough, Ashe had some Burgundy in the kitchen, and they took that with them in the taxi.

Dinner was very good and they drank both bottles of wine. Kiever opened up a little on the second: he'd just come back from a tour of West Germany and France. France was in a hell of a mess, de Gaulle was on the way out, and God alone knew what would happen then. With a hundred thousand demoralized *colons* returning from Algeria he reckoned fascism was in the cards.

"What about Germany?" asked Ashe, prompting him.

"It's just a question of whether the Yanks can hold them." Kiever looked invitingly at Leamas.

"What do you mean?" asked Leamas.

"What I say. Dulles gave them a foreign policy with one hand, Kennedy takes it away with the other. They're getting waspish."

Leamas nodded abruptly and said, "Bloody typical Yank."

"Alec doesn't seem to like our American cousins," said Ashe, stepping in heavily, and Kiever, with complete disinterest, murmured, "Oh really?"

Kiever played it, Leamas reflected, very long. Like someone used to horses, he let you come to him. He conveyed to perfection a man who suspected that he was about to be asked a favor, and was not easily won.

After dinner Ashe said, "I know a place in Wardour Street —you've been there, Sam. They do you all right there. Why don't we summon a cab and go along?"

"Just a minute," said Leamas, and there was something in his voice which made Ashe look at him quickly. "Just tell me something, will you? Who's paying for this jolly?"

"I am," said Ashe quickly. "Sam and I."

"Have you discussed it?"

"Well—no."

"Because I haven't got any bloody money; you know that, don't you? None to throw about, anyway."

"Of course, Alec. I've looked after you up till now, haven't I?"

"Yes," Leamas replied. "Yes, you have."

He seemed to be going to say something else, and then to change his mind. Ashe looked worried, not offended, and Kiever as inscrutable as before.

Leamas refused to speak in the taxi. Ashe attempted some conciliatory remark and he just shrugged irritably. They arrived at Wardour Street and dismounted, neither Leamas nor Kiever making any attempt to pay for the cab. Ashe led them past a shop window full of "girlie" magazines, down a narrow alley, at the far end of which shone a tawdry neon sign: Pussywillow Club—members only. On either side of the door were photographs of girls, and pinned across each was a thin, hand-printed strip of paper which read *Nature Study. Members Only.*

Ashe pressed the bell. The door was at once opened by a very large man in a white shirt and black trousers.

"I'm a member," Ashe said. "These two gentlemen are with me."

"See your card?"

Ashe took a buff card from his wallet and handed it over.

"Your guests pay a quid a head, temporary membership. Your recommendation, right?" He held out the card and as he did so, Leamas stretched past Ashe and took it. He looked at it for a moment, then handed it back to Ashe.

Taking two pounds from his hip pocket, Leamas put them into the waiting hand of the man at the door.

"Two quid," said Leamas, "for the guests," and ignoring the astonished protests of Ashe he guided them through the curtained doorway into the dim hallway of the club. He turned to the doorman.

"Find us a table," said Leamas, "and a bottle of Scotch. And see we're left alone."

The doorman hesitated for a moment, decided not to argue, and escorted them downstairs. As they descended they heard the subdued moan of unintelligible music. They got a table on their own at the back of the room. A two-piece band was playing and girls sat around in twos and threes. Two got up as they came in but the big doorman shook his head.

Ashe glanced at Leamas uneasily while they waited for the whisky. Kiever seemed slightly bored. The waiter brought a bottle and three tumblers and they watched in silence as he poured a little whisky into each glass. Leamas took the bottle from the waiter and added as much again to each. This done, he leaned across the table and said to Ashe, "Now perhaps you'll tell me what the bloody hell's going on."

"What do you mean?" Ashe sounded uncertain. "What *do* you mean, Alec?"

"You followed me from prison the day I was released," he began quietly, "with some bloody silly story of meeting me in Berlin. You gave me money you didn't owe me. You've bought me expensive meals and you're putting me up in your flat."

Ashe colored and said, "If that's the—"

"Don't interrupt," said Leamas fiercely. "Just damn well wait till I've finished, do you mind? Your membership card for this place is made out for someone called Murphy. Is that your name?"

"No, it is not."

"I suppose a friend called Murphy lent you his membership card?"

"No, he didn't as a matter of fact. If you must know, I

come here occasionally to find a girl. I used a phony name to join the club."

"Then why," Leamas persisted ruthlessly, "is Murphy registered as the tenant of your flat?"

It was Kiever who finally spoke.

"You run along home," he said to Ashe. "I'll look after this."

A girl performed a striptease, a young, drab girl with a dark bruise on her thigh. She had that pitiful, spindly naked-ness which is embarrassing because it is not erotic; because it is artless and undesiring. She turned slowly, jerking sporadi-cally with her arms and legs as if she only heard the music in snatches, and all the time she looked at them with the pre-cocious interest of a child in adult company. The tempo of the music increased abruptly, and the girl responded like a dog to the whistle, scampering back and forth. Removing her brassiere on the last note, she held it above her head, dis-playing her meager body with its three tawdry patches of tinsel hanging from it like old Christmas tree decorations.

They watched in silence, Leamas and Kiever.

"I suppose you're going to tell me that we've seen better in Berlin," Leamas suggested at last, and Kiever saw that he was still very angry.

"I expect *you* have," Kiever replied pleasantly. "I have often been to Berlin, but I am afraid I dislike night clubs."

Leamas said nothing.

"I'm no prude, mind, just rational. If I want a woman I know cheaper ways of finding one; if I want to dance I know better places to do it."

Leamas might not have been listening. "Perhaps you'll

tell me why that sissy picked me up," he suggested. Kiever nodded.

"By all means. I told him to."

"Why?"

"I am interested in you. I want to make you a proposition, a journalistic proposition."

There was a pause.

"Journalistic," Leamas repeated. "I see."

"I run an agency, an international feature service. It pays well—very well—for interesting material."

"Who publishes the material?"

"It pays so well, in fact, that a man with your kind of experience of . . . the international scene, a man with your background, you understand, who provided convincing, factual material, could free himself in a comparatively short time from further financial worry."

"Who publishes the material, Kiever?" There was a threatening edge to Leamas' voice, and for a moment, just for a moment, a look of apprehension seemed to pass across Kiever's smooth face.

"International clients. I have a correspondent in Paris who disposes of a good deal of my stuff. Often I don't even know who *does* publish. I confess," he added with a disarming smile, "that I don't awfully care. They pay and they ask for more. They're the kind of people, you see, Leamas, who don't fuss about awkward details; they pay promptly, and they're happy to pay into foreign banks, for instance, where no one bothers about things like tax."

Leamas said nothing. He was holding his glass with both hands, staring into it.

Christ, they're rushing their fences, Leamas thought; it's indecent. He remembered some silly music hall joke— 'This is an offer no respectable girl could accept—and besides, I don't know what it's worth." Tactically, he reflected, they're right to rush it. I'm down and out, prison experience still fresh, social resentment strong. I'm an old horse, I don't need breaking in; I don't have to pretend they've offended my honor as an English gentleman.

On the other hand they would expect *practical* objections. They would expect him to be afraid; for his Service pursued traitors as the eye of God followed Cain across the desert. And finally, they would know it was a gamble. They would know that inconsistency in human decision can make non-sense of the best-planned espionage approach; that cheats, liars and criminals may resist every blandishment while respectable gentlemen have been moved to appalling treasons by watery cabbage in a departmental canteen.

"They'd have to pay a hell of a lot," Leamas muttered at last. Kiever gave him some more whisky.

"They are offering a down payment of fifteen thousand pounds. The money is already lodged at the Banque Cantonale in Bern. On production of a suitable identification, with which my clients will provide you, you can draw the money. My clients reserve the right to put questions to you over the period of one year on payment of another five thousand pounds. They will assist you with any . . . resettlement problems that may arise."

"How soon do you want an answer?"

"Now. You are not expected to commit all your reminiscences to paper. You will meet my client and he will arrange to have the material . . . ghost written."

"Where am I supposed to meet him?"

"We felt for everybody's sake it would be simplest to meet outside the United Kingdom. My client suggested Holland."

"I haven't got my passport," Leamas said dully.

"I took the liberty of obtaining one for you," Kiever replied suavely; nothing in his voice or his manner indicated that he had done other than negotiate an adequate business arrangement. "We're flying to The Hague tomorrow morning at nine forty-five. Shall we go back to my flat and discuss any other details?"

Kiever paid and they took a taxi to a rather good address not far from St. James's Park.

Kiever's flat was luxurious and expensive, but its contents somehow gave the impression of having been hastily assembled. It is said there are shops in London which will sell you bound books by the yard, and interior decorators who will harmonize the color scheme of the walls with that of a painting. Leamas, who was not particularly receptive to such subtleties, found it hard to remember that he was in a private flat and not a hotel. As Kiever showed him to his room (which looked onto a dingy inner courtyard and not onto the street) Leamas asked him:

"How long have you been here?"

"Oh, not long," Kiever replied lightly, "a few months, not more."

"Must cost a packet. Still, I suppose you're worth it."

"Thanks."

There was a bottle of Scotch in his room and a syphon of soda on a silver-plated tray. A curtained doorway at the farther end of the room led to a bathroom and lavatory.

"Quite a little love nest. All paid for by the great Worker State?"

"Shut up," said Kiever savagely, and added, "If you want me, there's an intercom telephone to my room. I shall be awake."

"I think I can manage my buttons now," Leamas retorted.
"Then good night," said Kiever shortly, and left the room.
He's on edge, too, thought Leamas.

Leamas was awakened by the telephone at his bedside. It
was Kiever.
"It's six o'clock," he said, "breakfast at half past."
"All right," Leamas replied, and rang off. He had a headache.

Kiever must have telephoned for a taxi, because at seven
o'clock the doorbell rang and Kiever asked, "Got everything?"
"I've no luggage," Leamas replied, "except a toothbrush
and a razor."
"That is taken care of. Are you ready otherwise?"
Leamas shrugged. "I suppose so. Have you any cigarettes?"
"No," Kiever replied, "but you can get some on the plane.
You'd better look through this," he added, and handed Leamas a British passport. It was made out in his name with his
own photograph mounted in it, embossed by a deep-press
Foreign Office seal running across the corner. It was neither
old nor new; it described Leamas as a clerk, and gave his
status as single. Holding it in his hand for the first time, Leamas was a little nervous. It was like getting married: whatever happened, things would never be the same again.
"What about money?" Leamas asked.
"You don't need any. It's on the firm."

✠ ✠ 8 ✠ Le Mirage

It was cold that morning, the light mist was damp and gray, pricking the skin. The airport reminded Leamas of the war: machines, half hidden in the fog, waiting patiently for their masters; the resonant voices and their echoes, the sudden shout and the incongruous clip of a girl's heels on a stone floor; the roar of an engine that might have been at your elbow. Everywhere that air of conspiracy which generates among people who have been up since dawn —of superiority almost, from the common experience of having seen the night disappear and the morning come. The staff had that look which is informed by the mystery of dawn and animated by the cold, and they treated the passengers and their luggage with the remoteness of men returned from the front: ordinary mortals had nothing for them that morning.

Kiever had provided Leamas with luggage. It was a nice detail: Leamas admired it. Passengers without luggage attract attention, and it was not part of Kiever's plan to do that. They checked in at the airline desk and followed the signs to passport control. There was a ludicrous moment when they lost the way and Kiever was rude to a porter. Leamas supposed Kiever was worried about the passport— he needn't be, thought Leamas, there's nothing wrong with it.

The passport officer was a youngish little man with an Intelligence Corps tie and some mysterious badge in his lapel. He had a ginger mustache and a North Country accent which was his life's enemy.

"Going to be away for a long time, sir?" he asked Leamas.

"A couple of weeks," Leamas replied.

"You'll want to watch it, sir. Your passport's due for renewal on the thirty-first."

"I know," said Leamas.

They walked side by side into the passengers' waiting room. On the way Leamas said: "You're a suspicious sod, aren't you, Kiever?" and the other laughed quietly.

"Can't have you on the loose, can we? Not part of the contract," he replied.

They still had twenty minutes to wait. They sat down at a table and ordered coffee. "And take these things away," Kiever added to the waiter, indicating the used cups, saucers and ashtrays on the table.

"There's a trolley coming around," the waiter replied.

"Take them," Kiever repeated, angry again. "It's disgusting, leaving dirty dishes there like that."

The waiter just turned and walked away. He didn't go near the service counter and he didn't order their coffee. Kiever was white, ill with anger. "For Christ's sake," Leamas muttered, "let it go. Life's too short."

"Cheeky bastard, that's what he is," said Kiever.

"All right, all right, make a scene; you've chosen a good moment, they'll never forget us here."

The formalities at the airport at The Hague provided no problem. Kiever seemed to have recovered from his anxieties. He became jaunty and talkative as they walked the short distance between the plane and the customs sheds. The young Dutch officer gave a perfunctory glance at their luggage and passports and announced in awkward, throaty English, "I hope you have a pleasant stay in the Netherlands."

"Thanks," said Kiever, almost too gratefully, "thanks very much."

They walked from the customs shed along the corridor to the reception hall on the other side of the airport buildings. Kiever led the way to the main exit, between the little groups of travelers staring vaguely at kiosk displays of scent, cameras and fruit. As they pushed their way through the revolving glass door, Leamas looked back. Standing at the newspaper kiosk, deep in a copy of the *Continental Daily Mail*, stood a small, froglike figure wearing glasses, an earnest, worried little man. He looked like a civil servant. Something like that.

A car was waiting for them in the parking lot, a Volkswagen with a Dutch registration, driven by a woman who ignored them. She drove slowly, always stopping if the lights were amber, and Leamas guessed she had been briefed to drive that way and that they were being followed by another car. He watched the sideview mirror, trying to recognize the car but without success. Once he saw a black Peugeot with a CD number, but when they turned the corner there was only a furniture van behind them. He knew The Hague quite well from the war, and he tried to work out where they were heading. He guessed they were traveling northwest toward Scheveningen. Soon they had left the suburbs behind them and were approaching a colony of villas bordering the dunes along the seafront.

Here they stopped. The woman got out, leaving them in the car, and rang the front doorbell of a small cream-colored bungalow which stood at the near end of the row. A wrought-iron sign hung on the porch with the words LE MIRAGE in pale blue Gothic script. There was a notice in the window which proclaimed that all the rooms were taken.

The door was opened by a kindly, plump woman who looked past the driver toward the car. Her eyes still on the car, she came down the drive toward them, smiling with pleasure. She reminded Leamas of an old aunt he'd once had who beat him for wasting string.

"How nice that you have come," she declared; "we are so *pleased* that you have come!"

They followed her into the bungalow, Kiever leading the way. The driver got back into the car. Leamas glanced down the road which they had just traveled; three hundred yards away a black car, a Fiat perhaps, or a Peugeot, had parked. A man in a raincoat was getting out.

Once in the hall, the woman shook Leamas warmly by the hand. "Welcome, welcome to Le Mirage. Did you have a good journey?"

"Fine," Leamas replied.

"Did you fly or come by sea?"

"We flew," Kiever said; "a very smooth flight." He might have owned the airline.

"I'll make your lunch," she declared, "a special lunch. I'll make you something specially good. What shall I bring you?"

"Oh, for God's sake," said Leamas under his breath, and the doorbell rang. The woman went quickly into the kitchen; Kiever opened the front door.

He was wearing a mackintosh with leather buttons. He was about Leamas' height, but older. Leamas put him at about fifty-five. His face had a hard, gray hue and sharp furrows; he might have been a soldier. He held out his hand.

"My name is Peters," he said. The fingers were slim and polished. "Did you have a good journey?"

"Yes," said Kiever quickly, "quite uneventful."

"Mr. Leamas and I have a lot to discuss; I do not think we need to keep you, Sam. You could take the Volkswagen back to town."

Kiever smiled. Leamas saw the relief in his smile.

"Good-bye, Leamas," said Kiever, his voice jocular. "Good luck, old man."

Leamas nodded, ignoring Kiever's hand.

"Good-bye," Kiever repeated and let himself quietly out of the front door.

Leamas followed Peters into a back room. Heavy lace curtains hung at the window, ornately frilled and draped. The windowsill was covered with potted plants—great cacti, tobacco plant and some curious tree with wide, rubbery leaves. The furniture was heavy, pseudo-antique. In the center of the room was a table with two carved chairs. The table was covered with a rust-colored counterpane more like a carpet; on it before each chair was a pad of paper and a pencil. On a sideboard there was whisky and soda. Peters went over to it and mixed them both a drink.

"Look," said Leamas suddenly, "from now on I can do without the goodwill, do you follow me? We both know what we're about; both professionals. You've got a paid defector—good luck to you. For Christ's sake don't pretend you've fallen in love with me." He sounded on edge, uncertain of himself.

Peters nodded. "Kiever told me you were a proud man," he observed dispassionately. Then he added without smiling, "After all, why else does a man attack tradesmen?"

Leamas guessed he was Russian, but he wasn't sure. His English was nearly perfect, he had the ease and habits of a man long used to civilized comforts.

They sat at the table.

"Kiever told you what I am going to pay you?" Peters inquired.

"Yes. Fifteen thousand pounds to be drawn on a Bern bank."

"Yes."

"He said you might have follow-up questions during the next year," said Leamas. "You would pay another five thousand if I kept myself available."

Peters nodded.

"I don't accept that condition," Leamas continued. "You know as well as I do it wouldn't work. I want to draw the fifteen thousand and get clear. Your people have a rough way with defected agents; so have mine. I'm not going to sit on my fanny in St. Moritz while you roll up every network I've given you. They're not fools; they'd know who to look for. For all you and I know they're on to us now."

Peters nodded. "You could, of course, come somewhere . . . safer, couldn't you?"

"Behind the Curtain?"

"Yes."

Leamas just shook his head and continued: "I reckon you'll need about three days for a preliminary interrogation. Then you'll want to refer back for a detailed brief."

"Not necessarily," Peters replied.

Leamas looked at him with interest. "I see," he said, "they've sent the expert. Or isn't Moscow Centre in on this?"

Peters was silent; he was just looking at Leamas, taking him in. At last he picked up the pencil in front of him and said, "Shall we begin with your war service?"

Leamas shrugged.

"It's up to you."

"That's right. We'll begin with your war service. Just talk."

"I enlisted in the Engineers in 1939. I was finishing my training when a notice came around inviting linguists to apply for specialist service abroad. I had Dutch and German and a good deal of French and I was fed up with soldiering, so I applied. I knew Holland well; my father had a machine tool agency at Leiden; I'd lived there for nine years. I had the usual interviews and went off to a school near Oxford where they taught me the usual monkey tricks."

"Who was running that setup?"

"I didn't know till later. Then I met Steed-Asprey, and an Oxford don called Fielding. They were running it. In forty-one they dropped me into Holland and I stayed there nearly two years. We lost agents quicker than we could find them in those days—it was bloody murder. Holland's a wicked country for that kind of work—it's got no real rough country, nowhere out of the way you can keep a headquarters or a radio set. Always on the move, always running away. It made it a very dirty game. I got out in forty-three and had a couple of months in England, then I had a go at Norway— that was a picnic by comparison. In forty-five they paid me off and I came over here again, to Holland, to try and catch up on my father's old business. That was no good, so I joined up with an old friend who was running a travel agency business in Bristol. That lasted eighteen months, then we went bankrupt. Then out of the blue I got a letter from the Department: would I like to go back? But I'd had enough of all that, I thought, so I said I'd think about it and rented a cottage on Lundy Island. I stayed there a year contemplating my stomach, then I got fed up again so I wrote to them. By late forty-nine I was back on the payroll. Broken service, of course—reduction of pension rights and the usual crabbing. Am I going too fast?"

"Not for the moment," Peters replied, pouring him some more whisky. "We'll discuss it again of course, with names and dates."

There was a knock at the door and the woman came in with lunch, an enormous meal of cold meats and bread and soup. Peters pushed his notes aside and they ate in silence. The interrogation had begun.

Lunch was cleared away. "So you went back to the Circus," said Peters.

"Yes. For a while they gave me a desk job, processing

reports, making assessments of military strengths in Iron Curtain countries, tracing units and that kind of thing."

"Which section?"

"Satellites Four. I was there from February fifty to May fifty-one."

"Who were your colleagues?"

"Peter Guillam, Brian de Grey and George Smiley. Smiley left us in early fifty-one and went over to Counterintelligence. In May fifty-one I was posted to Berlin as D.C.A.—Deputy Controller of Area. That meant all the operational work."

"Who did you have under you?" Peters was writing swiftly. Leamas guessed he had some homemade shorthand.

"Hackett, Sarrow and de Jong. De Jong was killed in a traffic accident in fifty-nine. We thought he was murdered but we could never prove it. They all ran networks and I was in charge. Do you want details?" he asked drily.

"Of course, but later. Go on."

"It was late fifty-four when we landed our first big fish in Berlin: Fritz Feger, second man in the D.D.R. Defense Ministry. Up till then it had been heavy going—but in November fifty-four we got on to Fritz. He lasted almost exactly two years, then one day we never heard any more. I hear he died in prison. It was another three years before we found anyone to touch him. Then, in 1959, Karl Riemeck turned up. Karl was on the Praesidium of the East German Communist Party. He was the best agent I ever knew."

"He is now dead," Peters observed.

A look of something like shame passed across Leamas' face.

"I was there when he was shot," he muttered. "He had a mistress who came over just before he died. He'd told her everything—she knew the whole damned network. No wonder he was blown."

"We'll return to Berlin later. Tell me this. When Karl died you flew back to London. Did you remain in London for the rest of your service?"

"What there was of it, yes."

"What job did you have in London?"

"Banking section; supervision of agents' salaries, overseas payments for clandestine purposes. A child could have managed it. We got our orders and we signed the drafts. Occasionally there was a security headache."

"Did you deal with agents direct?"

"How could we? The Resident in a particular country would make a requisition. Authority would put a hoof-mark on it and pass it to us to make the payment. In most cases we had the money transferred to a convenient foreign bank where the Resident could draw it himself and hand it to the agent."

"How were agents described? By cover names?"

"By figures. The Circus calls them combinations. Every network was given a combination: every agent was described by a suffix attached to the combination. Karl's combination was eight A stroke one."

Leamas was sweating. Peters watched him coolly, appraising him like a professional gambler across the table. What was Leamas worth? What would break him, what attract or frighten him? What did he hate; above all, what did he know? Would he keep his best card to the end and sell it dear? Peters didn't think so: Leamas was too much off balance to monkey about. He was a man at odds with himself, a man who knew one life, one confession, and had betrayed them. Peters had seen it before. He had seen it, even in men who had undergone a complete ideological reversal, who in the secret hours of the night had found a new creed, and alone, compelled by the internal power of their convictions, had betrayed their calling, their families, their countries. Even they, filled as they were with new zeal and new hope, had had to struggle against the stigma of treachery; even they wrestled with the almost physical anguish of saying that which they had been trained never, never to reveal. Like apostates who feared to burn the Cross, they hesitated between the instinctive and the material; and Peters, caught in the same polarity, must give them comfort and destroy their pride. It was a situation of which they were both aware; thus Leamas had fiercely rejected a human relationship with Peters, for his pride precluded it. Peters knew that for those reasons Leamas would lie; lie perhaps only by omission, but lie all the same, for pride, from defiance or through the sheer perversity of his profession; and he, Peters, would have to nail the lies. He knew, too, that the very fact that Leamas was a professional could militate against his interests, for Leamas would select where Peters wanted no selection; Leamas would anticipate the type of intelligence which Peters required—and in doing so might pass by some casual scrap which could be of vital interest to the evaluators. To all that, Peters added the capricious vanity of an alcoholic wreck.

"I think," he said, "we will now take your Berlin service in some detail. That would be from May 1951 to March 1961. Have another drink."

Leamas watched him take a cigarette from the box on the table and light it. He noticed two things: that Peters was left-handed, and that once again he had put the cigarette in his mouth with the maker's name away from him, so that it burned first. It was a gesture Leamas liked: it indicated that Peters, like himself, had been on the run.

Peters had an odd face, expressionless and gray. The color must have left it long ago—perhaps in some prison in the early days of the Revolution—and now his features were formed and Peters would look like that till he died. Only the stiff gray hair might turn to white, but his face would not change. Leamas wondered vaguely what Peters' real name was, whether he was married. There was something very orthodox about him which Leamas liked. It was the orthodoxy of strength, of confidence. If Peters lied there would be a reason. The lie would be a calculated, necessary lie, far removed from the fumbling dishonesty of Ashe.

Ashe, Kiever, Peters; that was a progression in quality, in authority, which to Leamas was axiomatic of the hierarchy of an intelligence network. It was also, he suspected, a progression in ideology. Ashe the mercenary, Kiever the fellow traveler, and now Peters, for whom the end and the means were identical.

Leamas began to talk about Berlin. Peters seldom interrupted, seldom asked a question or made a comment, but when he did, he displayed a technical curiosity and *expertise* which entirely accorded with Leamas' own temperament. Leamas even seemed to respond to the dispassionate professionalism of his interrogator—it was something they had in common.

It had taken a long time to build a decent East Zone network from Berlin, Leamas explained. In the earlier days the city had been thronging with second-rate agents: intelligence was discredited and so much a part of the daily life of Berlin that you could recruit a man at a cocktail party, brief him over dinner and he would be blown by breakfast.

For a professional it was a nightmare: dozens of agencies, half of them penetrated by the opposition, thousands of loose ends; too many leads, too few sources, too little space to operate. They had their break with Feger in 1954, true enough. But by '56 when every Service department was screaming for high-grade intelligence, they were becalmed. Feger had spoiled them for second-rate stuff that was only one jump ahead of the news. They needed the real thing—and they had to wait another three years before they got it.

Then one day de Jong went for a picnic in the woods on the edge of East Berlin. He had a British military number plate on his car, which he parked, locked, on a gravel road beside the canal. After the picnic his children ran on ahead, carrying the basket. When they reached the car they stopped, hesitated, dropped the basket and ran back. Somebody had forced the car door—the handle was broken and the door was slightly open. De Jong swore, remembering that he had left his camera in the glove compartment. He went and examined the car. The handle had been forced; de Jong reckoned it had been done with a piece of steel tubing, the kind of thing you can carry in your sleeve. But the camera was still there, so was his coat, so were some parcels belonging to his wife. On the driving seat was a tobacco tin, and in the tin was a small nickel cartridge. De Jong knew exactly what it contained: it was the film cartridge of a subminiature camera, probably a Minox.

De Jong drove home and developed the film. It contained the minutes of the last meeting of the Praesidium of the East German Communist Party, the S.E.D. By an odd coincidence there was collateral from another source; the photographs were genuine.

Leamas took the case over then. He was badly in need of a success. He'd produced virtually nothing since arriving in Berlin, and he was getting past the usual age limit for full-time operational work. Exactly a week later he took de Jong's car to the same place and went for a walk.

It was a desolate spot that de Jong had chosen for his picnic: a strip of canal with a couple of shell-torn pillboxes, some parched, sandy fields, and on the eastern side a sparse pinewood lying about two hundred yards from the gravel road which bordered the canal. But it had the virtue of solitude—something that was hard to find in Berlin—and surveillance was impossible. Leamas walked in the woods. He made no attempt to watch the car because he did not know from which direction the approach might be made. If he was seen watching the car from the woods, the chances of retaining his informant's confidence were ruined. He need not have worried.

When he returned there was nothing in the car so he drove back to West Berlin, kicking himself for being a damned fool; the Praesidium was not due to meet for another fortnight. Three weeks later he borrowed de Jong's car and took a thousand dollars in twenties in a picnic case. He left the car unlocked for two hours and when he returned there was a tobacco tin in the glove compartment. The picnic case was gone.

The films were packed with first-grade documentary stuff. In the next six weeks he did it twice more, and the same thing happened.

Leamas knew he had hit a gold mine. He gave the source the cover name of "Mayfair" and sent a pessimistic letter to London. Leamas knew that if he gave London half an opening they would control the case direct, which he was desperately anxious to avoid. This was probably the only kind of operation which could save him from superannuation, and it was just the kind of thing that was big enough for

London to want to take over for itself. Even if he kept them at arm's length there was still the danger that the Circus would have theories, make suggestions, urge caution, demand action. They would want him to give only new dollar bills in the hope of tracing them, they would want the film cartridges sent home for examination, they would plan clumsy tailing operations and tell the Departments. Most of all they would want to tell the Departments; and that, said Leamas, would blow the thing sky-high. He worked like a madman for three weeks. He combed the personality files of each member of the Praesidium. He drew up a list of all the clerical staff who might have had access to the minutes. From the distribution list on the last page of the facsimiles he extended the total of possible informants to thirty-one, including clerks and secretarial staff.

Confronted with the almost impossible task of identifying an informant from the incomplete records of thirty-one candidates, Leamas returned to the original material, which, he said, was something he should have done earlier. It puzzled him that in none of the photostated minutes he had so far received were the pages numbered, that none was stamped with a security classification, and that in the second and fourth copies words were crossed out in pencil or crayon. He came finally to an important conclusion: that the photo copies related not to the minutes themselves, but to the *draft* minutes. This placed the source in the Secretariat and the Secretariat was very small. The draft minutes had been well and carefully photographed: that suggested that the photographer had had time and a room to himself.

Leamas returned to the personality index. There was a man called Karl Riemeck in the Secretariat, a former corporal in the Medical Corps, who had served three years as a prisoner of war in England. His sister had been living in

Pomerania when the Russians overran it, and he had never heard of her since. He was married and had one daughter named Carla.

Leamas decided to take a chance. He found out from London Riemeck's prisoner of war number, which was 29012, and the date of his release which was December 10, 1945. He bought an East German children's book of science fiction and wrote in the fly leaf in German in an adolescent hand: *This book belongs to Carla Riemeck, born December 10, 1945, in Bideford, North Devon. Signed Moonspacewoman 29012,* and underneath he added, *Applicants wishing to make space flights should present themselves for instruction to C. Riemeck in person. An application form is enclosed. Long Live the People's Republic of Democratic Space!*

He ruled some lines on a sheet of writing paper, made columns for name, address and age, and wrote at the bottom of the page:

> *Each candidate will be interviewed personally. Write to the usual address stating when and where you wish to be met. Applications will be considered in seven days.*
>
> C.R.

He put the sheet of paper inside the book. Leamas drove to the usual place, still in de Jong's car, and left the book on the passenger seat with five used one-hundred dollar bills inside the cover. When Leamas returned, the book was gone, and there was a tobacco tin on the seat instead. It contained three rolls of film. Leamas developed them that night: one film contained as usual the minutes of the Praesidium's last meeting; the second showed a draft revision of the East German relationship to COMECON; and the third was a breakdown of the East German Intelligence Service, complete with functions of departments and details of personalities.

Peters interrupted. "Just a minute," he said. "Do you mean to say all this intelligence came from Riemeck?"

"Why not? You know how much he saw."

"It's scarcely possible," Peters observed, almost to himself. "He must have had help."

"He did have later on; I'm coming to that."

"I know what you are going to tell me. But did you never have the feeling he got assistance from *above* as well as from the agents he afterwards acquired?"

"No. No, I never did. It never occurred to me."

"Looking back on it now, does it seem likely?"

"Not particularly."

"When you sent all this material back to the Circus, they never suggested that even for a man in Riemeck's position the intelligence was phenomenally comprehensive?"

"No."

"Did they ever ask where Riemeck got his camera from, who instructed him in document photography?"

Leamas hesitated.

"No . . . I'm sure they never asked."

"Remarkable," Peters observed drily. "I'm sorry—do go on. I did not mean to anticipate you."

Exactly a week later, Leamas continued, he drove to the canal and this time he felt nervous. As he turned into the gravel road he saw three bicycles lying in the grass and two hundred yards down the canal, three men fishing. He got out of the car as usual and began walking toward the line of trees on the other side of the field. He had gone about twenty yards when he heard a shout. He looked around and caught sight of one of the men beckoning to him. The other two had turned and were looking at him too. Leamas was wearing an old mackintosh; he had his hands in the pockets, and it was too late to take them out. He knew that the men on either side were covering the man in the middle and that if he took his hands out of his pockets they would probably shoot him; they would think he was holding a revolver in his pocket. Leamas stopped ten yards from the center man.

"You want something?" Leamas asked.

"Are you Leamas?" He was a small, plump man, very steady. He spoke English.

"Yes."

"What is your British national identity number?"

"PRT stroke L 58003 stroke one."

"Where did you spend VJ night?"

"At Leiden in Holland in my father's workshop, with some Dutch friends."

"Let's go for a walk, Mr. Leamas. You won't need your mackintosh. Take it off and leave it on the ground where you are standing. My friends will look after it."

Leamas hesitated, shrugged and took off his mackintosh. Then they walked together briskly toward the wood.

"You know as well as I do who he was," said Leamas wearily, "third man in the Ministry of the Interior, Secretary to the S.E.D. Praesidium, head of the Co-ordinating Committee for the Protection of the People. I suppose that was how he knew about de Jong and me: he'd seen our counterintelligence files in the Abteilung. He had three strings to his bow: the Praesidium, straightforward internal political and economic reporting, and access to the files of the East German Security Service."

"But only *limited* access. They'd never give an outsider the run of all their files," Peters insisted.

Leamas shrugged.

"They did," he said.

"What did he do with his money?"

"After that afternoon I didn't give him any. The Circus took that over straightaway. It was paid into a West German bank. He even gave me back what I'd given him. London banked it for him."

"How much did you tell London?"

"Everything after that. I had to; then the Circus told the Departments. After that," Leamas added venomously, "it was only a matter of time before it packed up. With the Departments at their backs, London got greedy. They began pressing us for more, wanted to give him more money. Finally we had to suggest to Karl that he recruit other sources, and we took them on to form a network. It was bloody stupid, it put a strain on Karl, endangered him, undermined his confidence in us. It was the beginning of the end."

"How much did you get out of him?"

Leamas hesitated. "How much? Christ, I don't know. It lasted an unnaturally long time. I think he was blown long before he was caught. The standard dropped in the last few months; think they'd begun to suspect him by then and kept him away from the good stuff."

"Altogether, what did he give you?" Peters persisted.

Piece by piece, Leamas recounted the full extent of all Karl Riemeck's work. His memory was, Peters noted approvingly, remarkably precise considering the amount he drank. He could give dates and names, he could remember the reaction from London, the nature of corroboration where it existed. He could remember sums of money demanded and paid, the dates of the conscription of other agents into the network.

"I'm sorry," said Peters at last, "but I do not believe that one man, however well placed, however careful, however industrious, could have acquired such a range of detailed knowledge. For that matter, even if he had he would never have been able to photograph it."

"He *was* able," Leamas persisted, suddenly angry. "He bloody well did and that's all there is to it."

"And the Circus never told you to go into it with him, exactly how and when he saw all this stuff?"

"No," snapped Leamas. "Riemeck was touchy about that, and London was content to let it go."

"Well, well," Peters mused.

After a moment Peters said, "You heard about that woman, incidentally?"

"What woman?" Leamas asked sharply.

"Karl Riemeck's mistress, the one who came over to West Berlin the night Riemeck was shot."

"Well?"

"She was found dead a week ago. Murdered. She was shot from a car as she left her flat."

"It used to be my flat," said Leamas mechanically.

"Perhaps," Peters suggested, "she knew more about Riemeck's network than you did."

"What the hell do you mean?" Leamas demanded.

Peters shrugged. "It's all very strange," he observed. "I wonder who killed her."

When they had exhausted the case of Karl Riemeck, Leamas went on to talk of other less spectacular agents, then of the procedure of his Berlin office, its communications, its staff, its secret ramifications—flats, transport, recording and photographic equipment. They talked long into the night and throughout the next day, and when at last Leamas stumbled into bed the following night he knew he had betrayed all that he knew of Allied Intelligence in Berlin and had drunk two bottles of whisky in two days.

One thing puzzled him: Peters' insistence that Karl Riemeck must have had help—must have had a high-level collaborator. Control had asked him the same question—he remembered now—Control had asked about Riemeck's access. How could they both be so sure Karl hadn't managed alone? He'd had helpers, of course; like the guards by the canal the day Leamas met him. But they were small beer—Karl had told him about them. But Peters—and Peters, after all, would know precisely how much Karl had been able to get his hands on—Peters had refused to believe Karl had managed alone. On this point, Peters and Control were evidently agreed.

Perhaps it was true. Perhaps there was somebody else. Perhaps this was the special interest whom Control was so anxious to protect from Mundt. That would mean that Karl Riemeck had collaborated with this special interest and provided what both of them had together obtained. Perhaps that was what Control had spoken to Karl about, alone, that evening in Leamas' flat in Berlin.

Anyway, tomorrow would tell. Tomorrow he would play his hand.

He wondered who had killed Elvira. And he wondered *why* they had killed her. Of course—here was a point, here was a possible explanation—Elvira, knowing the identity of Riemeck's special collaborator, had been murdered *by* that collaborator. . . . No, that was too farfetched. It overlooked the difficulty of crossing from East to West: Elvira had after all been murdered in West Berlin.

He wondered why Control had never told him Elvira had

been murdered. So that he would react suitably when Peters told him? It was useless speculating. Control had his reasons; they were usually so bloody tortuous it took you a week to work them out.

As he fell asleep he muttered, "Karl was a damn fool. That woman did for him, I'm sure she did." Elvira was dead now, and serve her right. He remembered Liz.

✠ ✠ 9 ✠ The Second Day

Peters arrived at eight o'clock the next morning, and without ceremony they sat down at the table and began.

"So you came back to London. What did you do there?"

"They put me on the shelf. I knew I was finished when that ass in Personnel met me at the airport. I had to go straight to Control and report about Karl. He was dead—what else was there to say?"

"What did they do with you?"

"They said at first I could hang around in London and wait till I was qualified for a proper pension. They were so bloody decent about it I got angry—I told them that if they were so keen to chuck money at me why didn't they do the obvious thing and count in all my time instead of bleating about broken service? Then they got cross when I told them that. They put me in Banking with a lot of women. I can't remember much about that part—I began hitting the bottle a bit. Went through a bad phase."

He lit a cigarette. Peters nodded.

"That was why they gave me the push, really. They didn't like me drinking."

"Tell me what you *do* remember about Banking Section," Peters suggested.

"It was a dreary setup. I never was cut out for desk work, I knew that. That's why I hung on in Berlin. I knew when they recalled me I'd be put on the shelf, but Christ!"

"What did you do?"

Leamas shrugged.

"Sat on my behind in the same room as a couple of women. Thursby and Larrett. I called them Thursday and Friday." He grinned rather stupidly. Peters looked uncomprehending.

"We just pushed paper. A letter came down from Finance: 'The payment of seven hundred dollars to so and so is authorized with effect from so and so. Kindly get on with it'— that was the gist of it. Thursday and Friday would kick it about a bit, file it, stamp it, and I'd sign a check or get the bank to make a transfer."

"What bank?"

"Blatt and Rodney, a chichi little bank in the City. There's a sort of theory in the Circus that Etonians are discreet."

"In fact, then, you knew the names of agents all over the world?"

"Not necessarily. That was the cunning thing. I'd sign the check, you see, or the order to the bank, but we'd leave a space for the name of the payee. The covering letter or what have you was all signed and then the file would go *back* to Special Dispatch."

"Who are they?"

"They're the general holders of agents' particulars. They

put in the names and posted the order. Bloody clever, I must say."

Peters looked disappointed.

"You mean you had no way of knowing the names of the payees?"

"Not usually, no."

"But occasionally?"

"We got pretty near the knuckle now and again. All the fiddling about between Banking, Finance and Special Dispatch led to cockups, of course. Too elaborate. Then occasionally we came in on special stuff which brightened one's life a bit."

Leamas got up. "I've made a list," he said, "of all the payments I can remember. It's in my room. I'll get it."

He walked out of the room, the rather shuffling walk he had affected since arriving in Holland. When he returned he held in his hand a couple of sheets of lined paper torn from a cheap notebook.

"I wrote these down last night," he said. "I thought it would save time."

Peters took the notes and read them slowly and carefully. He seemed impressed.

"Good," he said, "very good."

"Then I remember best a thing called Rolling Stone. I got a couple of trips out of it. One to Copenhagen and one to Helsinki. Just dumping money at banks."

"How much?"

"Ten thousand dollars in Copenhagen, forty thousand D-marks in Helsinki."

Peters put down his pencil.

"Who for?" he asked.

"God knows. We worked Rolling Stone on a system of deposit accounts. The Service gave me a phony British passport; I went to the Royal Scandinavian Bank in Copenhagen and the National Bank of Finland in Helsinki, deposited the money and drew a passbook on a joint account—for me in my alias and for someone else—the agent I suppose in his alias. I gave the banks a sample of the co-holder's signature, I'd got that from Head Office. Later, the agent was given the passbook and a false passport which he showed at the bank when he drew the money. All I knew was the alias." He heard himself talking and it all sounded so ludicrously improbable.

"Was this procedure common?"

"No. It was a special payment. It had a subscription list."

"What's that?"

"It had a code name known to very few people."

"What was the code name?"

"I told you—Rolling Stone. The operation covered irregular payments of ten thousand dollars in different currencies and in different capitals."

"Always in capital towns?"

"Far as I know. I remember reading in the file that there had been other Rolling Stone payments before I came to the Section, but in those cases Banking Section got the local Resident to do it."

"These other payments that took place before you came: where were they made?"

"One in Oslo. I can't remember where the other was."

"Was the alias of the agent always the same?"

"No. That was an added security precaution. I heard later we pinched the whole technique from the Russians. It was the most elaborate payment scheme I'd met. In the same way I used a different alias and of course a different passport for each trip." That would please him, help him to fill in the gaps.

"These faked passports the agent was given so that he could draw the money: did you know anything about them —how they were made out and dispatched?"

"No. Oh, except that they had to have visas in them for the country where the money was deposited. And entry stamps."

"*Entry stamps?*"

"Yes. I assumed the passports were never used at the border—only presented at the bank for identification purposes. The agent must have traveled on his own passport, quite legally entered the country where the bank was situated, then used the faked passport at the bank. That was my guess."

"Do you know of a reason why earlier payments were made by the Residents, and later payments by someone traveling out from London?"

"I know the reason. I asked the women in Banking Section, Thursday and Friday. Control was anxious that—"

"*Control?* Do you mean to say Control himself was running the case?"

"Yes, he was running it. He was afraid the Resident might be recognized at the bank. So he used a postman: me."

"When did you make your journeys?"

"Copenhagen on the fifteenth of June. I flew back the same night. Helsinki at the end of September. I stayed two nights there, flew back around the twenty-eighth. I had a bit of fun in Helsinki." He grinned but Peters took no notice.

"And the other payments—when were they made?"

"I can't remember. Sorry."

"But one was definitely in Oslo?"

"Yes, in Oslo."

"How much time separated the first two payments, the payments made by the Residents?"

"I don't know. Not long, I think. Maybe a month. A bit more perhaps."

"Was it your impression that the agent had been operating for some time before the first payment was made? Did the file show that?"

"No idea. The file simply covered actual payments. First payment early fifty-nine. There was no other date on it. That is the principle that operates where you have a limited subscription. Different files handle different bits of a single case. Only someone with the master file would be able to put it all together."

Peters was writing all the time now. Leamas assumed there was a tape recorder hidden somewhere in the room but the subsequent transcription would take time. What Peters wrote down now would provide the background for this evening's telegram to Moscow, while at the Soviet Embassy in The Hague the girls would sit up all night telegraphing the verbatim transcript on hourly schedules.

"Tell me," said Peters; "these are large sums of money. The arrangements for paying them were elaborate and very expensive. What did you make of it yourself?"

Leamas shrugged. "What could I make of it? I thought Control must have a bloody good source, but I never saw the material so I don't know. I didn't like the way it was done —it was too high-powered, too complicated, too clever. Why couldn't they just meet him and give him the money in cash? Did they really let him cross borders on his own passport with a forged one in his pocket? I doubt it," said Leamas. It was time he clouded the issue, let him chase a hare.

"What do you mean?"

"I mean, that for all I know the money was never drawn from the bank. Supposing he was a highly placed agent behind the Curtain—the money would be on deposit for him when he could get at it. That was what I reckoned anyway. I didn't think about it all that much. Why should I? It's part of our work only to know pieces of the whole setup. You know that. If you're curious, God help you."

"If the money wasn't collected, as you suggest, why all the trouble with passports?"

"When I was in Berlin we made an arrangement for Karl Riemeck in case he ever needed to run and couldn't get hold of us. We kept a bogus West German passport for him at an address in Düsseldorf. He could collect it any time by following a prearranged procedure. It never expired—Special Travel renewed the passport and the visas as they expired. Control might have followed the same technique with this man. I don't know—it's only a guess."

"How do you know for certain that passports were issued?"

"There were minutes on the file between Banking Section and Special Travel. Special Travel is the section which arranges false identity papers and visas."

"I see." Peters thought for a moment and then he asked: "What names did you use in Copenhagen and Helsinki?"

"Robert Lang, electrical engineer from Derby. That was in Copenhagen."

"When exactly were you in Copenhagen?" Peters asked.

"I told you, June the fifteenth. I got there in the morning at about eleven-thirty."

"Which bank did you use?"

"Oh, for Christ's sake, Peters," said Leamas, suddenly angry, "the Royal Scandinavian. You've got it written down."

"I just wanted to be sure," the other replied evenly, and continued writing. "And for Helsinki, what name?"

"Stephen Bennett, marine engineer from Plymouth. I was there," he added sarcastically, "at the end of September."

"You visited the bank on the day you arrived?"

"Yes. It was the twenty-fourth or twenty-fifth, I can't be sure, as I told you."

"Did you take the money with you from England?"

"Of course not. We just transferred it to the Resident's account in each case. The Resident drew it, met me at the airport with the money in a suitcase and I took it to the bank."

"Who's the Resident in Copenhagen?"

"Peter Jensen, a bookseller in the University bookshop."

"And what were the names which would be used by the agent?"

"Horst Karlsdorf in Copenhagen. I think that was it, yes it was, I remember. Karlsdorf. I kept on wanting to say Karlshorst."

"Description?"

"Manager, from Klagenfurt in Austria."

"And the other? The Helsinki name?"

"Fechtmann, Adolf Fechtmann from St. Gallen, Switzerland. He had a title—yes, that's right: Doctor Fechtmann, archivist."

"I see; both German-speaking."

"Yes, I noticed that. But it can't be a German."

"Why not?"

"I was head of the Berlin setup, wasn't I? I'd have been in on it. A high-level agent in East Germany would have to be run from Berlin. I'd have known." Leamas got up, went to the sideboard and poured himself some whisky. He didn't bother about Peters.

"You said yourself there were special precautions, special procedures in this case. Perhaps they didn't think you needed to know."

"Don't be bloody silly," Leamas rejoined shortly; "of course

I'd have known." This was the point he would stick to through thick and thin; it made them feel they knew better, gave credence to the rest of his information. "They will want to deduce *in spite of you,*" Control had said. "We must give them the material and remain skeptical to their conclusions. Rely on their intelligence and conceit, on their suspicion of one another—that's what we must do."

Peters nodded as if he were confirming a melancholy truth. "You are a very proud man, Leamas," he observed once more.

Peters left soon after that. He wished Leamas good day and walked down the road along the seafront. It was lunchtime.

⚔ ⚔ 10 ⚔ The Third Day

Peters didn't appear that afternoon, nor the next morning. Leamas stayed in, waiting with growing irritation for some message, but none came. He asked the housekeeper but she just smiled and shrugged her heavy shoulders. At about eleven o'clock the next morning he decided to go out for a walk along the front, bought some cigarettes and stared dully at the sea.

There was a girl standing on the beach throwing bread to the sea gulls. Her back was turned to him. The sea wind played with her long black hair and pulled at her coat, making an arc of her body, like a bow strung toward the sea. He knew then what it was that Liz had given him; the thing that he would have to go back and find if ever he got home to England: it was the caring about little things—the faith in ordinary life; that simplicity that made you break up a bit of bread into a paper bag, walk down to the beach and throw it to the gulls. It was this respect for triviality which he had never been allowed to possess; whether it was bread for the sea gulls or love, whatever it was he would go back and find it; he would make Liz find it for him. A week, two weeks perhaps, and he would be home. Control had said he could keep whatever they paid—and that would be enough. With fifteen thousand pounds, a gratuity and a pension from the Circus, a man—as Control would say—can afford to come in from the cold.

He made a detour and returned to the bungalow at a quarter to twelve. The woman let him in without a word, but when he had gone into the back room he heard her lift the receiver and dial a telephone number. She spoke for only a few seconds. At half-past twelve she brought his lunch, and, to his pleasure, some English newspapers which he read contentedly until three o'clock. Leamas, who normally read nothing, read newspapers slowly and with concentration. He remembered details, like the names and addresses of people who were the subject of small news items. He did it almost unconsciously as a kind of private Pelmanism, and it absorbed him entirely.

At three o'clock Peters arrived, and as soon as Leamas saw him he knew that something was up. They did not sit at the table; Peters did not take off his mackintosh.

"I've got bad news for you," he said. "They're looking for you in England. I heard this morning. They're watching the ports."

Leamas replied impassively, "On what charge?"

"Nominally for failing to report to a police station within the statutory period after release from prison."

"And in fact?"

"The word is going around that you're wanted for an offense under the Official Secrets Act. Your photograph's in all the London evening papers. The captions are very vague."

Leamas was standing very still.

Control had done it. Control had started the hue and cry. There was no other explanation. If Ashe or Kiever had been pulled in, if they had talked—even then, the responsibility for the hue and cry was still Control's. "A couple of weeks," he'd said; "I expect they'll take you off somewhere for the interrogation—it may even be abroad. A couple of weeks should see you through, though. After that, the thing should run itself. You'll have to lie low over here while the chemistry works itself out; but you won't mind that, I'm sure. I've agreed to keep you on operational subsistence until Mundt is eliminated: that seemed the fairest way."

And now this.

This wasn't part of the bargain; this was different. What the hell was he supposed to do? By pulling out now, by refusing to go along with Peters, he was wrecking the operation. It was just possible that Peters was lying, that this was the test—all the more reason that he should agree to go. But if he went, if he agreed to go east, to Poland, Czechoslovakia or God knows where, there was no good reason why they should ever let him out—there was no good reason (since he was notionally a wanted man in the West) why he should *want* to be let out.

Control had done it—he was sure. The terms had been too generous, he'd known that all along. They didn't throw money about like that for nothing—not unless they thought they might lose you. Money like that was a *douceur* for discomforts and dangers Control would not openly admit to. Money like that was a warning; Leamas had not heeded the warning.

"Now how the devil," he asked quietly, "could they get onto that?" A thought seemed to cross his mind and he said,

"Your friend Ashe could have told them, of course, or Kiever . . ."

"It's possible," Peters replied. "You know as well as I do that such things are always possible. There is no certainty in our job. The fact is," he added with something like impatience, "that by now every country in western Europe will be looking for you."

Leamas might not have heard what Peters was saying. "You've got me on the hook now, haven't you, Peters?" he said. "Your people must be laughing themselves sick. Or did they give the tip-off themselves?"

"You overrate your own importance," Peters said sourly.

"Then why do you have me followed, tell me that? I went for a walk this morning. Two little men in brown suits, one twenty yards behind the other, trailed me along the seafront. When I came back the housekeeper rang you up."

"Let us stick to what we know," Peters suggested. "How your own authorities have got on to you does not at the moment acutely concern us. The fact is, they have."

"Have you brought the London evening papers with you?"

"Of course not. They are not available here. We received a telegram from London."

"That's a lie. You know perfectly well your apparatus is only allowed to communicate with Centre."

"In this case a direct link between two outstations was permitted," Peters retorted angrily.

"Well, well," said Leamas with a wry smile, "you must be quite a big wheel. Or"—a thought seemed to strike him—"isn't Centre in on this?"

Peters ignored the question.

"You know the alternative. You let us take care of you, let us arrange your safe passage, or you fend for yourself— with the certainty of eventual capture. You've no false papers, no money, nothing. Your British passport will have expired in ten days."

"There's a third possibility. Give me a Swiss passport and some money and let me run. I can look after myself."

"I am afraid that is not considered desirable."

"You mean you haven't finished the interrogation. Until you have I am not expendable?"

"That is roughly the position."

"When you have completed the interrogation, what will you do with me?"

Peters shrugged. "What do you suggest?"

"A new identity. Scandinavian passport perhaps. Money."

"It's very academic," Peters replied, "but I will suggest it to my superiors. Are you coming with me?"

Leamas hesitated. Then he smiled a little uncertainly and asked, "If I didn't, what would you do? After all, I've quite a story to tell, haven't I?"

"Stories of that kind are hard to substantiate. I shall be gone tonight. Ashe and Kiever . . ." He shrugged. "What do they add up to?"

Leamas went to the window. A storm was gathering over the gray North Sea. He watched the gulls wheeling against the dark clouds. The girl had gone.

"All right," he said at last, "fix it up."

"There's no plane east until tomorrow. There's a flight to Berlin in an hour. We shall take that. It's going to be very close."

Leamas' passive role that evening enabled him once again to admire the unadorned efficiency of Peters' arrangements. The passport had been put together long ago—Centre must have thought of that. It was made out in the name of Alexander Thwaite, travel agent, and filled with visas and frontier stamps—the old, well-fingered passport of the professional traveler. The Dutch frontier guard at the airport just nodded and stamped it for form's sake—Peters was three or four behind him in the queue and took no interest in the formalities.

As they entered the "passengers only" enclosure Leamas caught sight of a bookstall. A selection of international newspapers was on show: *Figaro, Monde, Neue Zürcher Zeitung, die Welt,* and half a dozen British dailies and weeklies. As he watched, the girl came around to the front of the kiosk and pushed an *Evening Standard* into the rack. Leamas hurried across to the bookstall and took the paper from the rack.

"How much?" he asked. Thrusting his hand into his trouser pocket he suddenly realized that he had no Dutch currency.

"Thirty cents," the girl replied. She was rather pretty; dark and jolly.

"I've only got two English shillings. That's a guilder. Will you take them?"

"Yes, please," she replied, and Leamas gave her the florin. He looked back. Peters was still at the passport desk, his back turned. Without hesitation Leamas made straight for the men's lavatory. There he glanced rapidly but thoroughly at each page, then shoved the paper in the litter basket and re-emerged. It was true: there was his photograph with the vague little passage underneath. He wondered if Liz had seen it. He made his way thoughtfully to the passengers' lounge. Ten minutes later they boarded the plane for Hamburg and Berlin. For the first time since it all began, Leamas was frightened.

⌘ ⌘ 11 ⌘ Friends of Alec

The men called on Liz the same evening.

Liz Gold's room was at the northern end of Bayswater. It had a sofa-bed in it, and a gas fire—rather a pretty one in charcoal gray, which made a modern hiss instead of an old-fashioned bubble. She used to gaze into it sometimes when Leamas was there, when the gas fire shed the only light in the room. He would lie on the sofa, and she would sit beside him and kiss him, or watch the gas fire with her face pressed against his. She was afraid to think of him too much now because she had forgot what he looked like, so she let her mind think of him for brief moments like running her eyes across a faint horizon, and then she would remember some small thing he had said or done, some way he had looked at her, or more often, ignored her. That was the terrible thing, when her mind dwelled on it: she had nothing to remember him by—no photograph, no souvenir, nothing. Not even a mutual friend—only Miss Crail in the library, whose hatred of him had been vindicated by his spectacular departure. Liz had been around to his room once and seen the landlord. She didn't know why she did it quite, but she plucked up courage and went. The landlord was very kind about Alec; Mr. Leamas had paid his rent like a gentleman, right till the end, then there'd been a week or two owing and a chum of Mr. Leamas' had dropped in and paid up handsome, no queries or nothing. He'd always said it of Mr. Leamas, always would, he was a gent. Not public school, mind, nothing arsy-tarsy but a real gent. He liked to scowl a bit occasionally, and of course he drank a drop more than was good for him, though he never acted tight when he came home. But this little bloke who come round, funny little shy chap with specs, *he* said Mr. Leamas had particularly requested, quite particularly, that the rent owing should be settled up. And if *that* wasn't gentlemanly, the landlord was damned if he knew what was. Where he got the money from heaven knows, but that Mr. Leamas was a deep one and no mistake. He only did to Ford the grocer what a good many had been wanting to do ever since the war. The room? Yes, the room had been taken—a gentleman from Korea, two days after they took Mr. Leamas away.

That was probably why she went on working at the library —because there, at least, he still existed; the ladders, shelves, the books, the card index, were things he had known and touched, and one day he might come back to them. He had said he would never come back, but she didn't believe it. It was like saying you would never get better to believe a thing like that. Miss Crail thought he would come back: she ` had discovered she owed him some money—wages underpaid—and it infuriated her that her monster had been so unmonstrous as not to collect it. After Leamas had gone, Liz had never given up asking herself the same question;

why had he hit Mr. Ford? She knew he had a terrible temper, but that was different. He had intended to do it right from the start as soon as he had got rid of his fever. Why else had he said good-bye to her the night before? He knew that he would hit Mr. Ford on the following day. She refused to accept the only other possible interpretation: that he had grown tired of her and said good-bye, and the next day, still under the emotional strain of their parting, had lost his temper with Mr. Ford and struck him. She knew, she had always known, that there was something Alec had got to do. He'd even told her that himself. What it was she could only guess.

First, she thought he had a quarrel with Mr. Ford, some deep-rooted hatred going back for years. Something to do with a girl, or Alec's family perhaps. But you only had to look at Mr. Ford and it seemed ridiculous. He was the archetypal *petit-bourgeois*, cautious, complacent, mean. And anyway, if Alec had a vendetta on with Mr. Ford, why did he go for him in the shop on a Saturday, in the middle of the weekend shopping rush, when everyone could see?

They'd talked about it in the meeting of her Party branch. George Hanby, the branch treasurer, had actually been passing Ford the grocer's as it happened, he hadn't seen much because of the crowd but he'd talked to a bloke who'd seen the whole thing. Hanby had been so impressed that he'd rung the *Worker*, and they'd sent a man to the trial— that was why the *Worker* had given it a middle-page spread, as a matter of fact. It was just a straight case of protest—of sudden social awareness and hatred against the boss class, as the *Worker* said. This bloke that Hanby spoke to (he was just a little, ordinary chap with specs, white-collar type) said it had been so sudden—spontaneous was what he meant —and it just proved to Hanby once again how incendiary was the fabric of the capitalist system. Liz had kept very quiet while Hanby talked: none of them knew, of course, about her and Leamas. She realized then that she hated George Hanby; he was a pompous, dirty-minded little man, always leering at her and trying to touch her.

Then the men called.

She thought they were a little too smart for policemen: they came in a small black car with an aerial on it. One was short and rather plump. He had glasses and wore odd, expensive clothes; he was a kindly, worried little man and Liz trusted him somehow without knowing why. The other was smoother, but not glossy—rather a boyish figure, although she guessed he wasn't less than forty. They said they came from Special Branch, and they had printed cards with photographs in cellophane cases. The plump one did most of the talking.

"I believe you were friendly with Alec Leamas," he began. She was prepared to be angry, but the plump man was so earnest that it seemed silly.

"Yes," Liz answered. "How did you know?"

"We found out quite by chance the other day. When you go to . . . prison, you have to give next of kin. Leamas said he hadn't any. That was a lie, as a matter of fact. They asked him whom they should inform if anything happened to him in prison. He said you."

"I see."

"Does anyone else know you were friendly with him?"

"No."

"Did you go to the trial?"

"No."

"No press men called, creditors, no one at all?"

"No, I've told you. No one else knew. Not even my parents, no one. We worked together in the library, of course—the Psychical Research Library—but only Miss Crail, the librarian, would know that. I don't think it occurred to her that there was anything between us. She's queer," Liz added simply.

The little man peered very seriously at her for a moment, then he asked: "Did it surprise you when Leamas beat up Mr. Ford?"

"Yes, of course."

"Why do you think he did it?"

"I don't know. Because Ford wouldn't give him credit, I suppose. But I think he always meant to." She wondered if she was saying too much, but she longed to talk to somebody about it, she was so alone and there didn't seem any harm.

"But that night, the night before it happened, we talked together. We had supper, a sort of special one; Alec said we should and I knew that it was our last night. He'd got a bottle of red wine from somewhere; I didn't like it much, Alec drank most of it. And then I asked him, 'Is this good-bye'— whether it was all over."

"What did he say?"

"He said there was a job he'd got to do. Someone to pay off for something they'd done to a friend of his. I didn't really understand it all, not really."

There was a very long silence and the little man looked more worried than ever. Finally he asked her: "Do you believe that?"

"I don't know." She was suddenly terrified for Alec, and she didn't know why.

The man asked: "Leamas has got two children by his marriage, did he tell you?" Liz said nothing. "In spite of that he gave your name as next of kin. Why do you think he did that?" The little man seemed embarrassed by his own question. He was looking at his hands, which were pudgy and clasped together on his lap. Liz blushed.

"I was in love with him," she replied.

"Was he in love with you?"

"Perhaps. I don't know."

"Are you still in love with him?"

"Yes."

"Did he ever say he would come back?" asked the younger man.

"No."

"But he did say good-bye to you?" the other asked quickly.

"Did he say good-bye to you?" The little man repeated his question slowly, kindly. "Nothing more can happen to him, I promise you. But we want to help him, and if you have any idea of why he hit Ford, if you have the slightest notion from something he said, perhaps casually, or something he did, then tell us for Alec's sake."

Liz shook her head.

"Please go," she said, "please don't ask any more questions. Please go now."

As he got to the door, the elder man hesitated, then took a card from his wallet and put it on the table gingerly, as if it might make a noise. Liz thought he was a very shy little man.

"If you ever want any help—if anything happens about Leamas or—ring me up," he said. "Do you understand?"

"Who are you?"

"I'm a friend of Alec Leamas." He hesitated. "Another thing," he added, "one last question. Did Alec know you were . . . Did Alec know about the Party?"

"Yes," she replied hopelessly. "I told him."

"Does the Party know about you and Alec?"

"I've told you. No one knew." Then, white-faced, she cried out suddenly, "Where is he? Tell me where he is.

Why won't you tell me where he is? I can help him, don't you see; I'll look after him . . . even if he's gone mad, I don't care, I swear I don't. . . . I wrote to him in prison; I shouldn't have done that, I know. I just said he could come back any time, I'd wait for him always. . . ." She couldn't speak any more, just sobbed and sobbed, standing there in the middle of the room, her broken face buried in her hands; the little man watching her.

"He's gone abroad," he said gently. "We don't quite know where he is. He isn't mad, but he shouldn't have said all that to you. It was a pity."

The younger man said, "We'll see you're looked after. For money and that kind of thing."

"Who are you?" Liz asked again.

"Friends of Alec," the young man repeated; "good friends."

She heard them go quietly down the stairs and into the street. From her window she watched them get into a small black car and drive away in the direction of the park.

Then she remembered the card. Going to the table she picked it up and held it to the light. It was expensively done, more than a policeman could afford, she thought. Engraved. No rank in front of the name, no police station or anything. Just the name with "Mister"—and whoever heard of a policeman living in Chelsea?

MR. GEORGE SMILEY. 9 BYWATER STREET, CHELSEA. Then the telephone number underneath.

It was very strange.

✠ ✠ 12 ✠ East

Leamas unfastened his seat belt.

It is said that men condemned to death are subject to sudden moments of elation; as if, like moths in the fire, their destruction were coincidental with attainment. Following directly upon his decision, Leamas was aware of a comparable sensation; relief, short-lived but consoling, sustained him for a time. It was followed by fear and hunger.

He was slowing down. Control was right.

He'd noticed it first during the Riemeck Case early last year. Karl had sent a message: he'd got something special for him and was making one of his rare visits to West Germany; some legal conference at Karlsruhe. Leamas had managed to get an air passage to Cologne, and picked up a car at the airport. It was still quite early in the morning and he'd hoped to miss most of the autobahn traffic to Karlsruhe but the heavy lorries were already on the move. He drove seventy kilometers in half an hour, weaving between the traffic, taking risks to beat the clock, when a small

car, a Fiat probably, nosed its way out into the fast lane forty
yards ahead of him. Leamas stamped on the brake, turning his headlights full on and sounding his horn, and by the
grace of God he missed it; missed it by a fraction of a second. As he passed the car he saw out of the corner of his eye
four children in the back, waving and laughing, and the
stupid, frightened face of their father at the wheel. He drove
on, cursing, and suddenly it happened; suddenly his hands
were shaking feverishly, his face was burning hot, his heart
palpitating wildly. He managed to pull off the road into a
lay-by, scrambled out of the car and stood, breathing heavily, staring at the hurtling stream of giant lorries. He had a
vision of the little car caught among them, pounded and
smashed, until there was nothing left, nothing but the fre-
netic whine of klaxons and the blue lights flashing; and the
bodies of the children, torn, like the murdered refugees on
the road across the dunes.

He drove very slowly the rest of the way and missed his
meeting with Karl.

He never drove again without some corner of his memory
recalling the tousled children waving to him from the back
of that car, and their father grasping the wheel like a farmer
at the shafts of a hand plow.

Control would call it fever.

He sat dully in his seat over the wing. There was an American woman next to him wearing high-heeled shoes in poly-
thene wrappers. He had a momentary notion of passing her
some note for the people in Berlin, but he discarded it at
once. She'd think he was making a pass at her; Peters would
see it. Besides, what was the point? Control knew what had
happened; Control had made it happen. There was nothing
to say.

He wondered what would become of him. Control hadn't talked about that—only about the technique:

"Don't give it to them all at once, make them work for it. Confuse them with detail, leave things out, go back on your tracks. Be testy, be cussed, be difficult. Drink like a fish; don't give way on the ideology, they won't trust that. They want to deal with a man they've bought; they want the clash of opposites, Alec, not some half-cock convert. Above all, they want to *deduce*. The ground's prepared; we did it long ago, little things, difficult clues. You're the last stage in the treasure hunt."

He'd had to agree to do it: you can't back out of the big fight when all the preliminary ones have been fought for you.

"One thing I can promise you: it's worth it. It's worth it for our special interest, Alec. Keep him alive and we've won a great victory."

He didn't think he could stand torture. He remembered a book by Koestler where the old revolutionary had conditioned himself for torture by holding lighted matches to his fingers. He hadn't read much but he'd read that and he remembered it.

It was nearly dark when they landed at Templehof. Leamas watched the lights of Berlin rise to meet them, felt the thud as the plane touched down, saw the customs and immigration officials move forward out of the half-light.

For a moment Leamas was anxious lest some former acquaintance should chance to recognize him at the airport. As they walked side by side, Peters and he, along the interminable corridors, through the cursory customs and immigration check, and still no familiar face turned to greet him, he realized that his anxiety had in reality been hope; hope that somehow his tacit decision to go on would be revoked by circumstance.

It interested him that Peters no longer bothered to disown him. It was as if Peters regarded West Berlin as safe ground, where vigilance and security could be relaxed; a mere technical staging post to the East.

They were walking through the big reception hall to the main entrance when Peters suddenly seemed to alter his mind, abruptly changed direction and led Leamas to a smaller side entrance which gave on to a parking lot and taxi stand. There Peters hesitated a second, standing beneath the light over the door, then put his suitcase on the ground beside him, deliberately removed his newspaper from beneath his arm, folded it, pushed it into the left pocket of his raincoat and picked up his suitcase again. Immediately from the direction of the parking lot a pair of headlights sprang to life, were dipped and then extinguished.

"Come on," said Peters and started to walk briskly across the tarmac, Leamas following more slowly. As they reached the first row of cars the rear door of a black Mercedes was opened from the inside, and the courtesy light went on. Peters, ten yards ahead of Leamas, went quickly to the car, spoke softly to the driver, then called to Leamas.

"Here's the car. Be quick."

It was an old Mercedes 180 and he got in without a word. Peters sat beside him in the back. As they pulled out they overtook a small DKW with two men sitting in the front. Twenty yards down the road there was a telephone booth. A man was talking into the telephone, and he watched them go by, talking all the time. Leamas looked out of the back window and saw the DKW following them. Quite a reception, he thought.

They drove very slowly. Leamas sat with his hands on his knees, looking straight in front of him. He didn't want to see Berlin that night. This was his last chance, he knew that. The way he was sitting now he could drive the side of his right hand into Peters' throat, smashing the promontory of the thorax. He could get out and run, weaving to avoid the bullets from the car behind. He would be free—there were people in Berlin who would take care of him—he could get away.

He did nothing.

It was so easy crossing the sector border. Leamas had never expected it to be quite that easy. For about ten minutes they dawdled, and Leamas guessed that they had to cross at a prearranged time. As they approached the West German checkpoint, the DKW pulled out and overtook them with the ostentatious roar of a labored engine, and stopped at the police hut. The Mercedes waited thirty yards behind. Two minutes later the red and white pole lifted to let through the DKW and as it did so both cars drove over together, the Mercedes engine screaming in second gear, the driver pressing himself back against his seat, holding the wheel at arm's length.

As they crossed the fifty yards which separated the two checkpoints, Leamas was dimly aware of the new fortification on the eastern side of the wall—dragons' teeth, observation towers and double aprons of barbed wire. Things had tightened up.

The Mercedes didn't stop at the second checkpoint; the booms were already lifted and they drove straight through, the Vopos just watching them through binoculars. The DKW had disappeared, and when Leamas sighted it ten minutes later it was behind them again. They were driving fast now —Leamas had thought they would stop in East Berlin, change cars perhaps, and congratulate one another on a successful operation, but they drove on eastward through the city.

"Where are we going?" he asked Peters.

"We are there. The German Democratic Republic. They have arranged accommodation for you."

"I thought we'd be going further east."

"We are. We are spending a day or two here first. We thought the Germans ought to have a talk with you."

"I see."

"After all, most of your work has been on the German side. I sent them details from your statement."

"And they asked to see me?"

"They've never had anything quite like you, nothing quite so . . . near the source. My people agreed that they should have the chance to meet you."

"And from there? Where do we go from Germany?"

"East again."

"Who will I see on the German side?"

"Does it matter?"

"Not particularly. I know most of the Abteilung people by name, that's all. I just wondered."

"Who would you expect to meet?"

"Fiedler," Leamas replied promptly, "deputy head of security. Mundt's man. He does all the big interrogations. He's a bastard."

"Why?"

"A savage little bastard. I've heard about him. He caught an agent of Peter Guillam's and bloody nearly killed him."

"Espionage is not a cricket game," Peters observed sourly, and after that they sat in silence. So it is Fiedler, Leamas thought.

Leamas knew Fiedler, all right. He knew him from the photographs on the file and the accounts of his former subordinates. A slim, neat man, quite young, smooth-faced. Dark hair, bright brown eyes; intelligent and savage, as Leamas had said. A lithe, quick body containing a patient, retentive mind; a man seemingly without ambition for himself but remorseless in the destruction of others. Fiedler was a rarity in the Abteilung—he took no part in its intrigues, seemed content to live in Mundt's shadow without prospect of promotion. He could not be labeled as a member of this or that clique; even those who had worked close to him in the Abteilung could not say where he stood in its power complex. Fiedler was a solitary; feared, disliked and mistrusted. Whatever motives he had were concealed beneath a cloak of destructive sarcasm.

"Fiedler is our best bet," Control had explained. They'd been sitting together over dinner—Leamas, Control and Peter Guillam—in the dreary little seven-dwarfs' house in Surrey where Control lived with his beady wife, surrounded by carved Indian tables with brass tops. "Fiedler is the acolyte who one day will stab the high priest in the back. He's the only man who's a match for Mundt—" here Guillam had nodded—"and he hates his guts. Fiedler's a Jew of course, and Mundt is quite the other thing. Not at all a good mixture. It has been our job," he declared, indicating Guillam and himself, "to give Fiedler the weapon with which to destroy Mundt. It will be yours, my dear Leamas, to encourage him to use it. Indirectly, of course, because you'll never meet him. At least I certainly hope you won't."

They'd all laughed then, Guillam too. It had seemed a good joke at the time: good by Control's standards anyway.

It must have been after midnight.

For some time they had been traveling an unpaved road, partly through a wood and partly across open country. Now they stopped and a moment later the DKW drew up beside them. As he and Peters got out Leamas noticed that there were now three people in the second car. Two were already getting out. The third was sitting in the back seat looking at some papers by the light from the car roof, a slight figure half in shadow.

They had parked by some disused stables; the building lay thirty yards back. In the headlights of the car Leamas had glimpsed a low farmhouse with walls of timber and white-washed brick. The moon was up, and shone so brightly that the wooded hills behind were sharply defined against the pale night sky. They walked to the house, Peters and Leamas leading and the two men behind. The other man in the second car had still made no attempt to move; he remained there, reading.

As they reached the door Peters stopped, waiting for the other two to catch up. One of the men carried a bunch of keys in his left hand, and while he fiddled with them the other stood off, his hands in his pockets, covering him.

"They're taking no chances," Leamas observed to Peters. "What do they think I am?"

"They are not paid to think," Peters replied, and turning to one of them he asked in German, "Is he coming?"

The German shrugged and looked back toward the car. "He'll come," he said; "he likes to come alone."

They went into the house, the man leading the way. It was got up like a hunting lodge, part old, part new. It was badly lit with pale overhead lights. The place had a neglected, musty air as if it had been opened for the occasion. There were little touches of officialdom here and there—a notice of what to do in case of fire, institutional green paint on the door and heavy spring-cartridge locks; and in the drawing room, which was quite comfortably done, dark, heavy furniture, badly scratched, and the inevitable photographs of Soviet leaders. To Leamas these lapses from anonymity signified the involuntary identification of the Abteilung with bureaucracy. That was something he was familiar with in the Circus.

Peters sat down, and Leamas did the same. For ten minutes, perhaps longer, they waited, then Peters spoke to one of the two men standing awkwardly at the other end of the room.

"Go and tell him we're waiting. And find us some food, we're hungry." As the man moved toward the door Peters called, "And whisky—tell them to bring whisky and some glasses." The man gave an uncooperative shrug of his heavy shoulders and went out, leaving the door open behind him.

"Have you been here before?" asked Leamas.

"Yes," Peters replied, "several times."

"What for?"

"This kind of thing. Not the same, but our kind of work."

"With Fiedler?"

"Yes."

"Is he good?"

Peters shrugged. "For a Jew, he's not bad," he replied, and Leamas, hearing a sound from the other end of the room, turned and saw Fiedler standing in the doorway. In one hand he held a bottle of whisky, and in the other, glasses and some mineral water. He couldn't have been more than five foot six. He wore a dark blue single-breasted suit; the jacket was cut too long. He was sleek and slightly animal; his eyes were brown and bright. He was not looking at them but at the guard beside the door.

"Go away," he said. He had a slight Saxonian twang. "Go away and tell the other one to bring us food."

"I've told him," Peters called; "they know already. But they've brought nothing."

"They are great snobs," Fiedler observed drily in English. "They think we should have servants for the food."

Fiedler had spent the war in Canada. Leamas remembered that, now that he detected the accent. His parents had been German Jewish refugees, Marxists, and it was not until 1946 that the family returned home, anxious to take part, whatever the personal cost, in the construction of Stalin's Germany.

"Hello," he added to Leamas, almost by the way, "glad to see you."

"Hello, Fiedler."

"You've reached the end of the road."

"What the hell do you mean?" asked Leamas quickly.

"I mean that contrary to anything Peters told you, you are not going farther east. Sorry." He sounded amused.

Leamas turned to Peters.

"Is this true?" His voice was shaking with rage. "Is it true? Tell me!"

Peters nodded. "Yes. I am the go-between. We had to do it that way. I'm sorry," he added.

"Why?"

"*Force majeure,*" Fiedler put in. "Your initial interrogation took place in the West, where only an embassy could provide the kind of link we needed. The German Democratic Republic has no embassies in the West. Not yet. Our liaison section therefore arranged for us to enjoy facilities and communications and immunities which are at present denied to us."

"You bastard," hissed Leamas, "you lousy bastard! You knew I wouldn't trust myself to your rotten Service; that was the reason, wasn't it? That was why you used a Russian."

"We used the Soviet Embassy at The Hague. What else could we do? Up till then it was our operation. That's perfectly reasonable. Neither we nor anyone else could have known that your own people in England would get onto you so quickly."

"No? Not even when you put them on to me yourselves? Isn't that what happened, Fiedler? Well, isn't it?" Always remember to dislike them, Control had said. Then they will treasure what they get out of you.

"That is an absurd suggestion," Fiedler replied shortly. Glancing toward Peters he added something in Russian. Peters nodded and stood up.

"Good-bye," he said to Leamas. "Good luck."

He smiled wearily, nodded to Fiedler, then walked to the door. He put his hand on the door handle, then turned and called to Leamas again: "Good luck." He seemed to want Leamas to say something, but Leamas might not have heard. He had turned very pale, he held his hands loosely across his body, the thumbs upwards as if he were going to fight. Peters remained standing at the door.

"I should have known," said Leamas, and his voice had the odd, faulty note of a very angry man. "I should have guessed you'd never have the guts to do your own dirty work, Fiedler. It's typical of your rotten little half-country and your squalid little Service that you get big uncle to do your pimping for you. You're not a country at all, you're not a government, you're a fifth-rate dictatorship of political neurotics." Jabbing his finger in Fiedler's direction he shouted:

"I know you, you sadistic bastard, it's typical of you. You were in Canada in the war, weren't you? A bloody good place to be then, wasn't it? I'll bet you stuck your fat head into Mummy's apron any time an airplane flew over. What are you now? A creeping little acolyte to Mundt and twenty-two Russian divisions sitting on your mother's doorstep. Well, I pity you, Fiedler, the day you wake up and find them gone. There'll be a killing then, and not Mummy or big uncle will save you from getting what you deserve."

Fiedler shrugged.

"Regard it as a visit to the dentist, Leamas. The sooner it's all done, the sooner you can go home. Have some food and go to bed."

"You know perfectly well I can't go home," Leamas retorted. "You've seen to that. You blew me sky high in England, you had to, both of you. You knew damn well I'd never come here unless I had to."

Fiedler looked at his thin, strong fingers.

"This is hardly the time to philosophize," he said, "but you can't really complain, you know. All our work—yours and mine—is rooted in the theory that the whole is more important than the individual. That is why a Communist sees his secret service as the natural extension of his arm, and that is why in your own country intelligence is shrouded in a kind of *pudeur anglaise*. The exploitation of individuals can only be justified by the collective need, can't it? I find it slightly ridiculous that you should be so indignant. We are not here to observe the ethical laws of English country life. After all," he added silkily, "your own behavior has not, from the purist's point of view, been irreproachable."

Leamas was watching Fiedler with an expression of disgust.

"I know your setup. You're Mundt's poodle, aren't you? They say you want his job. I suppose you'll get it now. It's time the Mundt dynasty ended; perhaps this is it."

"I don't understand," Fiedler replied.

"I'm your big success, aren't I?" Leamas sneered.

Fiedler seemed to reflect for a moment, then he shrugged and said, "The operation was successful. Whether you were worth it is questionable. We shall see. But it was a good operation. It satisfied the only requirement of our profession: it worked."

"I suppose you take the credit?" Leamas persisted, with a glance in the direction of Peters.

"There is no question of credit," Fiedler replied crisply, "none at all." He sat down on the arm of the sofa, looked at Leamas thoughtfully for a moment and then said:

"Nevertheless, you are right to be indignant about one thing. Who told your people we had picked you up? We didn't. You may not believe me, but it happens to be true. We didn't tell them. We didn't even want them to know. We had ideas then of getting you to work for us later—ideas which I now realize to be ridiculous. So who told them? You were lost, drifting around, you had no address, no ties, no friends. Then how the devil did they know you'd gone? Someone told them—scarcely Ashe or Kiever, since they are both now under arrest."

"Under arrest?"

"So it appears. Not specifically for their work on your case, but there were other things. . . ."

"Well, well."

"It is true, what I said just now. We would have been content with Peters' report from Holland. You could have had your money and gone. But you hadn't told us everything; and I want to know everything. After all, your presence here provides us with problems too, you know."

"Well, you've boobed. I know damn all—and you're welcome to it."

There was a silence, during which Peters, with an abrupt and by no means friendly nod in Fiedler's direction, quietly let himself out of the room.

Fiedler picked up the bottle of whisky and poured a little into each glass.

"We have no soda, I'm afraid," he said. "Do you like water? I ordered soda, but they brought some wretched lemonade."

"Oh, go to hell," said Leamas. He suddenly felt very tired. Fiedler shook his head.

"You are a very proud man," he observed, "but never mind. Eat your supper and go to bed."

One of the guards came in with a tray of food—black bread, sausage and cold green salad.

"It is a little crude," said Fiedler, "but quite satisfying. No potato, I'm afraid. There is a temporary shortage of potatoes."

They began eating in silence, Fiedler very carefully, like a man who counted his calories.

The guards showed Leamas to his bedroom. They let him carry his own luggage—the same luggage that Kiever had given him before he left England—and he walked between them along the wide central corridor which led through the house from the front door. They came to a large double door, painted dark green, and one of the guards unlocked it; they beckoned to Leamas to go first. He pushed open the door and found himself in a small barrack bedroom with two bunk beds, a chair and a rudimentary desk. It was like something in prison camp. There were pictures of girls on the walls and the windows were shuttered. At the far end of the room was another door. They signaled him forward again. Putting down his baggage, he went and opened the door. The second room was identical to the first, but there was one bed and the walls were bare.

"You bring those cases," he said. "I'm tired." He lay on the bed, fully dressed, and within a few minutes he was fast asleep.

A sentry woke him with breakfast: black bread and *ersatz* coffee. He got out of bed and went to the window.

The house stood on a high hill. The ground fell steeply away from beneath his window, the crowns of pine trees visible above the crest. Beyond them, spectacular in their symmetry, unending hills, heavy with trees, stretched into the distance. Here and there a timber gully or firebreak formed a thin brown divide between the pines, seeming like Aaron's rod miraculously to hold apart massive seas of encroaching. forest. There was no sign of man; not a house or church, not even the ruin of some previous habitation—only the road, the yellow dirt road, a crayon line across the basin of the valley. There was no sound. It seemed incredible that anything so vast could be so still. The day was cold but clear. It must have rained in the night; the ground was moist, and the whole landscape so sharply defined against the white sky that Leamas could distinguish even single trees on the farthest hills.

He dressed slowly, drinking the sour coffee meanwhile. He

had nearly finished dressing and was about to start eating the bread when Fiedler came into the room.

"Good morning," he said cheerfully. "Don't let me keep you from your breakfast." He sat down on the bed. Leamas had to hand it to Fiedler; he had guts. Not that there was anything brave about coming to see him—the sentries, Leamas supposed, were still in the adjoining room. But there was an endurance, a defined purpose in his manner which Leamas could sense and admire.

"You have presented us with an intriguing problem," Fiedler observed.

"I've told you all I know."

"Oh no." He smiled. "Oh no, you haven't. You have told us all you are *conscious* of knowing."

"Bloody clever," Leamas muttered, pushing his food aside and lighting a cigarette—his last.

"Let me ask *you* a question," Fiedler suggested with the exaggerated bonhomie of a man proposing a party game. "As an experienced intelligence officer, what would *you* do with the information you have given us?"

"What information?"

"My dear Leamas, you have only given us one piece of intelligence. You have told us about Riemeck: we knew about Riemeck. You have told us about the dispositions of your Berlin organization, about its personalities and its agents. That, if I may say so, is old hat. Accurate—yes. Good background, fascinating reading, here and there good collateral, here and there a little fish which we shall take out of the pool. But not —if I may be crude—not fifteen thousand pounds' worth of intelligence. Not," he smiled again, "at current rates."

"Listen," said Leamas, "I didn't propose this deal—you did. You, Kiever and Peters. I didn't come crawling to your sissy friends, peddling old intelligence. You people made the running, Fiedler; you named the price and took the risk. Apart from that, I haven't had a bloody penny. So don't blame me if the operation's a flop." Make them come to you, Leamas thought.

"It isn't a flop," Fiedler replied, "it isn't finished. It can't be. You haven't told us what you *know*. I said you had given us one piece of intelligence. I'm talking about Rolling Stone. Let me ask you again—what would *you* do if I, if Peters or someone like us, had told *you* a similar story?"

Leamas shrugged. "I'd feel uneasy," he said. "It's happened before. You get an indication, several perhaps, that there's a spy in some department or at a certain level. So what? You can't arrest the whole government service. You can't lay traps for a whole department. You just sit tight and hope for more. You bear it in mind. In Rolling Stone you can't even tell what country he's working in."

"You are an operator, Leamas," Fiedler observed with a laugh, "not an evaluator. That is clear. Let me ask you some elementary questions."

Leamas said nothing.

"The file—the actual file on operation Rolling Stone. What color was it?"

"Gray with a red cross on it—that means limited subscription."

"Was anything attached to the outside?"

"Yes, the Caveat. That's the subscription label. With a legend saying that any unauthorized person not named on this label finding the file in his possession must at once return it unopened to Banking Section."

"Who was on the subscription list?"

"For Rolling Stone?"

"Yes."

"P.A. to Control, Control, Control's secretary; Banking

Section, Miss Bream of Special Registry and Satellites Four. That's all, I think. And Special Dispatch, I suppose—I'm not sure about them."

"Satellites Four? What do they do?"

"Iron Curtain countries excluding the Soviet Union and China. The Zone."

"You mean the GDR?"

"I mean the Zone."

"Isn't it unusual for a whole section to be on a subscription list?"

"Yes, it probably is. I wouldn't know—I've never handled limited subscription stuff before. Except in Berlin, of course; it was all different there."

"Who was in Satellites Four at that time?"

"Oh, God. Guillam, Haverlake, de Jong, I think. De Jong was just back from Berlin."

"Were they *all* allowed to see this file?"

"I don't know, Fiedler," Leamas retorted irritably, "and if I were you . . ."

"Then isn't it odd that a whole section was on the subscription list while all the rest of the subscribers are individuals?"

"I tell you I don't know—how could I know? I was just a clerk in all this."

"Who carried the file from one subscriber to another?"

"Secretaries, I suppose—I can't remember. It's bloody months since . . ."

"Then why weren't the secretaries on the list? Control's secretary was." There was a moment's silence.

"No, you're right; I remember now," Leamas said, a note of surprise in his voice. "We passed it by hand."

"Who else in Banking dealt with that file?"

"No one. It was my pigeon when I joined the Section. One

of the women had done it before, but when I came I took it over and they were taken off the list."

"Then you alone passed the file by hand to the next reader?"

"Yes . . . yes, I suppose I did."

"To whom did you pass it?"

"I . . . I can't remember."

"Think!" Fiedler had not raised his voice, but it contained a sudden urgency which took Leamas by surprise.

"To Control's P.A., I think, to show what action we had taken or recommended."

"Who brought the file?"

"What do you mean?" Leamas sounded off balance.

"Who brought you the file to read? Somebody on the list must have brought it to you."

Leamas' fingers touched his cheek for a moment in an involuntary nervous gesture.

"Yes, they must. It's difficult, you see, Fiedler; I was putting back a lot of drink in those days." His tone was oddly conciliatory. "You don't realize how hard it is to . . ."

"I ask you again. Think. Who brought you the file?"

Leamas sat down at the table and shook his head.

"I can't remember. It may come back to me. At the moment I just can't remember, really I can't. It's no good chasing it."

"It can't have been Control's girl, can it? You always handed the file *back* to Control's P.A. You said so. So those on the list must all have seen it *before* Control."

"Yes, that's it, I suppose."

"Then there is Special Registry, Miss Bream."

"She was just the woman who ran the strong room for subscription list files. That's where the file was kept when it wasn't in action."

"Then," said Fiedler silkily, "it must have been Satellites Four who brought it, mustn't it?"

"Yes, I suppose it must," said Leamas helplessly, as if he were not quite up to Fiedler's brilliance.

"Which floor did Satellites Four work on?"

"The second."

"And Banking?"

"The fourth. Next to Special Registry."

"Do you remember *who* brought it up? Or do you remember, for instance, going downstairs ever to collect the file from them?"

In despair, Leamas shook his head. Then suddenly he turned to Fiedler and cried: "Yes, yes I do! Of course I do! I got it from Peter!" Leamas seemed to have waked up: his face was flushed, excited. "That's it: I once collected the file from Peter in his room. We chatted together about Norway. We'd served there together, you see."

"Peter Guillam?"

"Yes, Peter—I'd forgotten about him. He'd come back from Ankara a few months before. He was on the list! Peter was—of course! That's it. It was Satellites Four and PG in brackets, Peter's initials. Someone else had done it before and Special Registry had glued a bit of white paper over the old name and put in Peter's initials."

"What territory did Guillam cover?"

"The Zone. East Germany. Economic stuff; ran a small section, sort of backwater. He was the chap. He brought the file up to me once too, I remember that now. He didn't run agents though. I don't quite know how he came into it— Peter and a couple of others were doing some research job on food shortages. Evaluation really."

"Did you not discuss it with him?"

"No, that's taboo. It isn't done with subscription files, I got

a homily from the woman in Special Registry about it—
Bream—no discussion, no questions."

"But taking into account the elaborate security precautions
surrounding Rolling Stone, it is possible, is it not, that Guillam's so-called research job might have involved the partial
running of this agent, Rolling Stone?"

"I've told Peters," Leamas almost shouted, banging his fist
on the desk, "it's just bloody silly to imagine that any operation could have been run against East Germany without my
knowledge—without the knowledge of the Berlin organization. I would have known, don't you see? How many times
do I have to say that? I would have known!"

"Quite so," said Fiedler softly, "of course you would." He
stood up and went to the window.

"You should see it in the autumn," he said, looking out.
"It's magnificent when the beeches are on the turn."

✠ ✠ 13 ✠ Pins or Paper Clips

Fiedler loved to ask questions. Sometimes, because he was a lawyer, he asked them for his own pleasure alone, to demonstrate the discrepancy between evidence and perfective truth. He possessed, however, that persistent inquisitiveness which for journalists and lawyers is an end in itself.

They went for a walk that afternoon, following the gravel road down into the valley, then branching into the forest along a broad, pitted track lined with felled timber. All the time, Fiedler probed, giving nothing. About the building in Cambridge Circus, and the people who worked there. What social class did they come from, what parts of London did they inhabit, did husbands and wives work in the same Departments? He asked about the pay, the leave, the morale, the canteen; he asked about their love-life, their gossip, their philosophy. Most of all he asked about their philosophy.

To Leamas that was the most difficult question of all.

"What do you mean, a philosophy?" he replied. "We're not Marxists, we're nothing. Just people."

"Are you Christians then?"

"Not many, I shouldn't think. I don't know many."

"What makes them do it, then?" Fiedler persisted: "They must have a philosophy."

"Why must they? Perhaps they don't know; don't even care. Not everyone has a philosophy," Leamas answered, a little helplessly.

"Then tell me what is your philosophy?"

"Oh for Christ's sake," Leamas snapped, and they walked on in silence for a while. But Fiedler was not to be put off.

"If they do not know what they want, how can they be so certain they are right?"

"Who the hell said they were?" Leamas replied irritably.

"But what is the justification then? What is it? For us it is easy, as I said to you last night. The Abteilung and organizations like it are the natural extension of the Party's arm. They are in the vanguard of the fight for Peace and Progress. They are to the Party what the Party is to socialism: they *are* the vanguard. Stalin said so—" he smiled drily, "it is not fashionable to quote Stalin—but he said once 'Half a million liquidated is a statistic, and one man killed in a traffic accident is a national tragedy.' He was laughing, you see, at the bourgeois sensitivities of the mass. He was a great cynic. But what he meant is still true: a movement which protects itself against counterrevolution can hardly stop at the exploitation—or the elimination, Leamas—of a few individuals. It is all one, we have never pretended to be wholly just in the process of rationalizing society. Some Roman said it, didn't he, in the Christian Bible—it is expedient that one man should die for the benefit of many?"

"I expect so," Leamas replied wearily.

"Then what do you think? What is your philosophy?"

"I just think the whole lot of you are bastards," said Leamas savagely.

Fiedler nodded. "That is a viewpoint I understand. It is primitive, negative and very stupid—but it is a viewpoint, it exists. But what about the rest of the Circus?"

"I don't know. How should I know?"

"Have you never discussed philosophy with them?"

"No. We're not Germans." He hesitated, then added vaguely· "I suppose they don't like Communism."

"And that justifies, for instance, the taking of human life? That justifies the bomb in the crowded restaurant; that justifies your write-off rate of agents—all that?"

Leamas shrugged. "I suppose so."

"You see, for us it does," Fiedler continued. "I myself would have put a bomb in a restaurant if it brought us farther along the road. Afterwards I would draw the balance—so many women, so many children; and so far along the road. But Christians—and yours is a Christian society—Christians may not draw the balance."

"Why not? They've got to defend themselves, haven't they?"

"But they believe in the sanctity of human life. They believe every man has a soul which can be saved. They believe in sacrifice."

"I don't know. I don't much care," Leamas added. "Stalin didn't either, did he?"

Fiedler smiled. "I like the English," he said, almost to himself; "my father did too. He was very fond of the English."

"That gives me a nice, warm feeling," Leamas retorted and lapsed into silence.

They stopped while Fiedler gave Leamas a cigarette and lit it for him.

They were climbing steeply now. Leamas liked the exercise, walking ahead with long strides, his shoulders thrust forward. Fiedler followed, slight and agile, like a terrier behind his master. They must have been walking for an hour, perhaps more, when suddenly the trees broke above them and the sky appeared. They had reached the top of a small hill, and could look down on the solid mass of pine broken only here and there by gray clusters of beach. Across the valley Leamas could glimpse the hunting lodge, perched below the crest of the opposite hill, low and dark against the trees. In the middle of the clearing was a rough bench beside a pile of logs and the damp remnants of a charcoal fire.

"We'll sit down for a moment," said Fiedler, "then we must go back." He paused. "Tell me: this money, these large sums in foreign banks—what did you think they were for?"

"What do you mean? I've told you, they were payments to an agent."

"An agent from behind the Iron Curtain?"

"Yes, I thought so," Leamas replied wearily.

"Why did you think so?"

"First, it was a hell of a lot of money. Then the complications of paying him; the special security. And of course, Control being mixed up in it."

"What do you think the agent did with the money?"

"Look, I've told you—I don't know. I don't even know if he collected it. I didn't know anything—I was just the bloody office boy."

"What did you do with the passbooks for the accounts?"

"I handed them in as soon as I got back to London—together with my phony passport."

"Did the Copenhagen or Helsinki banks ever write to you in London—to your alias, I mean?"

"I don't know. I suppose any letters would have been passed straight to Control anyway."

"The false signatures you used to open the accounts—Control had a sample of them?"

"Yes. I practiced them a lot and they had samples."

"More than one?"

"Yes. Whole pages."

"I see. Then letters could have gone to the banks after you had opened the accounts. You need not have known. The signatures could have been forged and the letters sent without your knowledge."

"Yes. That's right. I suppose that's what happened. I signed a lot of blank sheets too. I always assumed someone else took care of the correspondence."

"But you never did actually *know* of such correspondence?"

Leamas shook his head. "You've got it all wrong," he said, "you've got it all out of proportion. There was a lot of paper going around—this was just part of the day's work. It wasn't something I gave much thought to. Why should I? It was hush-hush, but I've been in on things all my life where you only know a little and someone else knows the rest. Besides, paper bores me stiff. I didn't lose any sleep over it. I liked the trips of course—I drew operational subsistence which helped. But I didn't sit at my desk all day, wondering about Rolling Stone. Besides," he added a little shamefacedly, "I was hitting the bottle a bit."

"So you said," Fiedler commented, "and of course, I believe you."

"I don't give a damn whether you believe me or not," Leamas rejoined hotly.

Fiedler smiled.

"I am glad. That is your virtue," he said, "that is your

great virtue. It is the virtue of indifference. A little resentment here, a little pride there, but that is nothing: the distortions of a tape recorder. You are objective. It occurred to me," Fiedler continued after a slight pause, "that you could still help us to establish whether any of that money was ever drawn. There is nothing to stop you writing to each bank and asking for a current statement. We could say you were staying in Switzerland; use an accommodation address. Do you see any objection to that?"

"It might work. It depends on whether Control has been corresponding with the bank independently, over my forged signature. It might not fit in."

"I do not see that we have much to lose."

"What have you got to win?"

"If the money has been drawn, which I agree is doubtful, we shall know where the agent was on a certain day. That seems to be a useful thing to know."

"You're dreaming. You'll never find him, Fiedler, not on that kind of information. Once he's in the West he can go to any consulate, even in a small town and get a visa for another country. How are you any the wiser? You don't even know whether the man is East German. What are you after?"

Fiedler did not answer at once. He was gazing distractedly across the valley.

"You said you are accustomed to knowing only a little, and I cannot answer your question without telling you what you should not know." He hesitated: "But Rolling Stone was an operation against us, I can assure you."

"Us?"

"The GDR." He smiled. "The Zone if you prefer. I am not really so sensitive."

He was watching Fiedler now, his brown eyes resting on him reflectively.

"But what about me?" Leamas asked. "Suppose I don't write the letters?" His voice was rising. "Isn't it time to talk about me, Fiedler?"

Fiedler nodded. "Why not?" he replied, agreeably.

There was a moment's silence, then Leamas said, "I've done my bit, Fiedler. You and Peters between you have got all I know. I never agreed to write letters to banks—it could be bloody dangerous, a thing like that. That doesn't worry you, I know. As far as you're concerned I'm expendable."

"Now let me be frank," Fiedler replied. "There are, as you know, two stages in the interrogation of a defector. The first stage in your case is nearly complete: you have told us all we can reasonably record. You have not told us whether your Service favors pins or paper clips because we haven't asked you, and because you did not consider the answer worth volunteering. There is a process on both sides of unconscious selection. Now it is always possible—and this is the worrying thing, Leamas—it is always entirely possible that in a month or two we shall unexpectedly and quite desperately need to know about the pins and paper clips. That is normally accounted for in the second stage—that part of the bargain which you refused to accept in Holland."

"You mean you're going to keep me on ice?"

"The profession of defector," Fiedler observed with a smile, "demands great patience. Very few are suitably qualified."

"How long?" Leamas insisted.

Fiedler was silent.

"Well?"

Fiedler spoke with sudden urgency. "I give you my word that as soon as I possibly can, I will tell you the answer to your question. Look—I could lie to you, couldn't I? I could say one month or less, just to keep you sweet. But I am telling you I don't know because that is the truth. You have given us some indications: until we have run them to earth I cannot listen to talk of letting you go. But afterwards, if things are as I think they are, you will need a friend and that friend will be me. I give you my word as a German."

Leamas was so taken aback that for a moment he was silent.

"All right," he said finally, "I'll play, Fiedler, but if you are stringing me along, somehow I'll break your neck."

"That may not be necessary," Fiedler replied evenly.

A man who lives a part, not to others but alone, is exposed to obvious psychological dangers. In itself, the practice of deception is not particularly exacting; it is a matter of experience, of professional *expertise,* it is a facility most of us can acquire. But while a confidence trickster, a play-actor or a gambler can return from his performance to the ranks of his admirers, the secret agent enjoys no such relief. For him, deception is first a matter of self-defense. He must protect himself not only from without but from within, and against the most natural of impulses: though he earn a fortune, his role may forbid him the purchase of a razor; though he be erudite, it can befall him to mumble nothing but banalities; though he be an affectionate husband and father, he must under all circumstances withhold himself from those in whom he should naturally confide.

Aware of the overwhelming temptations which assail a man permanently isolated in his deceit, Leamas resorted to the course which armed him best; even when he was alone, he compelled himself to live with the personality he had assumed. It is said that Balzac on his deathbed inquired anxiously after the health and prosperity of characters he had created. Similarly Leamas, without relinquishing the power of invention, identified himself with what he had invented.

The qualities he exhibited to Fiedler, the restless uncertainty, the protective arrogance concealing shame, were not approximations but extensions of qualities he actually possessed; hence also the slight dragging of the feet, the aspect of personal neglect, the indifference to food, and an increasing reliance on alcohol and tobacco. When alone, he remained faithful to these habits. He would even exaggerate them a little, mumbling to himself about the iniquities of his Service.

Only very rarely, as now, going to bed that evening, did he allow himself the dangerous luxury of admitting the great lie he lived.

Control had been phenomenally right. Fiedler was walking, like a man led in his sleep, into the net which Control had spread for him. It was uncanny to observe the growing identity of interest between Fiedler and Control: it was as if they had agreed on the same plan, and Leamas had been dispatched to fulfill it.

Perhaps that was the answer. Perhaps Fiedler was the special interest Control was fighting so desperately to preserve. Leamas didn't dwell on that possibility. He did not want to know. In matters of that kind he was wholly uninquisitive: he knew that no conceivable good could come of his deductions. Nevertheless, he hoped to God it was true. It was possible, just possible in that case, that he would get home.

✠ ✠ 14 ✠ Letter to a Client

Leamas was still in bed the next morning when Fiedler brought him the letters to sign. One was on the thin blue writing paper of the Seiler Hotel Alpenblick, Lake Spiez, Switzerland, the other from the Palace Hotel, Gstaad.

Leamas read the first letter:

To THE MANAGER,
The Royal Scandinavian Bank Ltd.,
Copenhagen.

DEAR SIR,

I have been traveling for some weeks and have not received any mail from England. Accordingly I have not had your reply to my letter of March 3rd requesting a current statement of the deposit account of which I am a joint signatory with Herr Karlsdorf. To avoid further delay, would you be good enough to forward a duplicate statement to me at the following address, where I shall be staying for two weeks beginning April 21st:

> c/o Madame Y. de Sanglot,
> 13 Avenue des Colombes,
> Paris XII,
> France.

I apologize for this confusion,

> Yours faithfully,
>
> (ROBERT LANG)

"What's all this about a letter of March third?" he asked. "I didn't write them any letter."

"No, you didn't. As far as we know, no one did. That will worry the bank. If there is any inconsistency between the letter we are sending them now and letters they have had from Control, they will assume the solution is to be found in the *missing* letter of March third. Their reaction will be to send you the statement as you ask, with a covering note regretting that they have not received your letter of the third."

The second letter was the same as the first; only the names were different. The address in Paris was the same. Leamas took a blank piece of paper and his fountain pen and wrote half a dozen times in a fluent hand "Robert Lang," then signed the first letter. Sloping his pen backwards he practiced the second signature until he was satisfied with it, then wrote "Stephen Bennett" under the second letter.

"Admirable," Fiedler observed, "quite admirable."

"What do we do now?"

"They will be posted in Switzerland tomorrow, in Interlaken and Gstaad. Our people in Paris will telegraph the replies to me as soon as they arrive. We shall have the answer in a week."

"And until then?"

"We shall be constantly in one another's company. I know that is distasteful to you, and I apologize. I thought we could go for walks, drive around in the hills a bit, kill time. I want you to relax and talk; talk about London, about Cambridge Circus and working in the Department; tell me the gossip, talk about the pay, the leave, the rooms, the paper and the people. The pins and the paper clips. I want to know all the little things that don't matter. Incidentally . . ." A change of tone.

"Yes?"

"We have facilities here for people who . . . for people who are spending some time with us. Facilities for diversion and so on."

"Are you offering me a woman?" he asked.

"Yes."

"No thank you. Unlike you, I haven't reached the stage where I need a pimp."

Fiedler seemed indifferent to his reply. He went on quickly.

"But you had a woman in England didn't you—the girl in the library?"

Leamas turned on him, his hands open at his sides.

"One thing!" he shouted. "Just that one thing—don't ever mention that again, not as a joke, not as a threat, not even to turn the screws, Fiedler, because it won't work, not ever; I'd dry up, do you see, you'd never get another bloody word from me as long as I lived. Tell that to them, Fiedler, to Mundt and Stammberger or whichever little alley-cat told you to say it—tell them what I said."

"I'll tell them," Fiedler replied. "I'll tell them. It may be too late."

In the afternoon they went walking again. The sky was dark and heavy, and the air warm.

"I've only been to England once," Fiedler observed casually. "That was on my way to Canada, with my parents before the war. I was a child then of course. We were there for two days."

Leamas nodded.

"I can tell you this now," Fiedler continued. "I nearly went there a few years back. I was going to replace Mundt on the Steel Mission—did you know he was once in London?"

"I knew," Leamas replied cryptically.

"I always wondered what it would have been like, that job."

"Usual game of mixing with the other Bloc Missions, I suppose. Certain amount of contact with British business —not much of that." Leamas sounded bored.

"But Mundt got about all right: he found it quite easy."

"So I hear," said Leamas; "he even managed to kill a couple of people."

"So you heard about that too?"

"From Peter Guillam. He was in on it with George Smiley. Mundt bloody nearly killed George as well."

"The Fennan Case," Fiedler mused. "It was amazing that Mundt managed to escape at all, wasn't it?"

"I suppose it was."

"You wouldn't think that a man whose photograph and personal particulars were filed at the Foreign Office as a member of a Foreign Mission would have a chance against the whole of British Security."

"From what I hear," Leamas said, "they weren't too keen to catch him anyway."

Fiedler stopped abruptly. "What did you say?"

"Peter Guillam told me he didn't reckon they wanted to catch Mundt, that's all I said. We had a different setup then —an Adviser instead of an Operational Control—a man called Maston. Maston had made a bloody awful mess of the Fennan Case from the start, that's what Guillam said. Peter reckoned that if they'd caught Mundt it would have made a hell of a stink—they'd have tried him and probably hanged him. The dirt that came out in the process would have finished Maston's career. Peter never knew quite what happened, but he was bloody sure there was no full-scale search for Mundt."

"You are sure of that, you are sure Guillam told you that in so many words? No full-scale search?"

"Of course I am sure."

"Guillam never suggested any other reason why they might have let Mundt go?"

"What do you mean?"

Fiedler shook his head and they walked on along the path.

"The Steel Mission was closed down after the Fennan Case," Fiedler observed a moment later, "that's why I didn't go."

"Mundt must have been mad. You may be able to get away with assassination in the Balkans—or here—but not London."

"He did get away with it though, didn't he?" Fiedler put in quickly. "And he did good work."

"Like recruiting Kiever and Ashe? God help him."

"They ran the Fennan woman for long enough."

Leamas shrugged.

"Tell me something else about Karl Riemeck," Fiedler began again. "He met Control once, didn't he?"

"Yes, in Berlin about a year ago, maybe a bit more."

"Where did they meet?"

"We all met together in my flat."

"Why?"

"Control loved to come in on success. We'd got a hell of

a lot of good stuff from Karl—I suppose it had gone down well with London. He came out on a short trip to Berlin and asked me to fix it up for them to meet."

"Did you mind?"

"Why should I?"

"He was your agent. You might not have liked him to meet other operators."

"Control isn't an operator, he's head of Department. Karl knew that and it tickled his vanity."

"Were you all three together, all the time?"

"Yes. Well, not quite. I left them alone for quarter of an hour or so—not more. Control wanted that—he wanted a few minutes alone with Karl, God knows why, so I left the flat on some excuse, I forget what. Oh—I know, I pretended we'd run out of Scotch. I actually went and collected a bottle from de Jong, in fact."

"Do you know what passed between them while you were out?"

"How could I? I wasn't that interested, anyway."

"Didn't Karl tell you afterwards?"

"I didn't ask him. Karl was a cheeky sod in some ways, always pretending he had something over me. I didn't like the way he sniggered about Control. Mind you, he had every right to snigger—it was a pretty ridiculous performance. We laughed about it together a bit, as a matter of fact. There wouldn't have been any point in pricking Karl's vanity; the whole meeting was supposed to give him a shot in the arm."

"Was Karl depressed then?"

"No, far from it. He was spoiled already. He was paid too much, loved too much, trusted too much. It was partly my fault, partly London's. If we hadn't spoiled him he wouldn't have told that bloody woman of his about his network."

"Elvira?"

"Yes."

They walked on in silence for a while, until Fiedler interrupted his own reverie to observe: "I'm beginning to like you. But there's one thing that puzzles me. It's odd—it didn't worry me before I met you."

"What's that?"

"Why you ever came. Why you defected." Leamas was going to say something when Fiedler laughed. "I'm afraid that wasn't very tactful, was it?" he said.

They spent that week walking in the hills. In the evenings they would return to the lodge, eat a bad meal washed down with a bottle of rank white wine, sit endlessly over their Steinhäger in front of the fire. The fire seemed to be Fiedler's idea—they didn't have it to begin with, then one day Leamas overheard him telling a guard to bring logs. Leamas didn't mind the evenings then; after the fresh air all day, the fire and the rough spirits, he would talk unprompted, rambling on about his Service. Leamas supposed it was recorded. He didn't care.

As each day passed in this way Leamas was aware of an increasing tension in his companion. Once they went out in the DKW—it was late in the evening—and stopped at a telephone booth. Fiedler left him in the car with the keys and made a long phone call.

When he came back Leamas said, "Why didn't you ring from the house?" but Fiedler just shook his head. "We must take care," he replied; "you too, you must take care."

"Why? What's going on?"

"The money you paid into the Copenhagen bank—we wrote, you remember?"

"Of course I remember."

Fiedler wouldn't say any more, but drove on in silence into the hills. There they stopped. Beneath them, half screened by the ghostly patchwork of tall pine trees, lay the meeting point of two great valleys. The steep wooded hills on either side gradually yielded their colors to the gathering dusk until they stood gray and lifeless in the twilight.

"Whatever happens," Fiedler said, "don't worry. It will be all right, do you understand?" His voice was heavy with emphasis, his slim hand rested on Leamas' arm. "You may have to look after yourself a little, but it won't last long, do you understand?" he asked again.

"No. And since you won't tell me, I shall have to wait and see. Don't worry too much for my skin, Fiedler." He moved his arm, but Fiedler's hand still held him. Leamas hated being touched.

"Do you know Mundt?" asked Fiedler. "Do you know about him?"

"We've talked about Mundt."

"Yes," Fiedler repeated, "we've talked about him. He shoots first and asks questions afterwards. The deterrent principle. It's an odd system in a profession where the questions are always supposed to be more important than the shooting." Leamas knew what Fiedler wanted to tell him. "It's an odd system unless you're frightened of the answers," Fiedler continued under his breath.

Leamas waited. After a moment Fiedler said, "He's never taken on an interrogation before. He's left it to me before, always. He used to say to me, 'You interrogate them, Jens, no one can do it like you. I'll catch them and you make them sing.' He used to say that people who do counterespionage are like painters—they need a man with a hammer standing behind them to strike when they have finished their work, otherwise they forget what they're trying to achieve. 'I'll be your hammer,' he used to say to me. It was a joke between us at first, then it began to matter; when he began to kill, kill them before they sang, just as you said: one here, another there, shot or murdered. I asked him, I begged him, 'Why not arrest them? Why not let me have them for a month or two? What good to you are they when they are dead?' He just shook his head at me and said there was a law that thistles must be cut down before they flower. I had the feeling that he'd prepared the answer before I ever asked the question. He's a good operator, very good. He's done wonders with the Abteilung—you know that. He's got theories about it; I've talked to him late at night. Coffee he drinks—nothing else—just coffee all the time. He says Germans are too introspective to make good agents, and it all comes out in counterintelligence. He says counterintelligence people are like wolves chewing dry bones—you have to take away the bones and make them find new quarry—I see all that, I know what he means. But he's gone too far. Why did he kill Viereck? Why did he take him away from me? Viereck was fresh quarry, we hadn't even taken the meat from the bone, you see. So why did he take him? Why, Leamas, why?" The hand on Leamas' arm was clasping it tightly; in the total darkness of the car Leamas was aware of the frightening intensity of Fiedler's emotion.

"I've thought about it night and day. Ever since Viereck was shot, I've asked for a reason. At first it seemed fantastic. I told myself I was jealous, that the work was going to my head, that I was seeing treachery behind every tree; we get like that, people in our world. But I couldn't help myself, Leamas, I had to work it out. There'd been other things before. He was afraid—he was afraid that we would catch one who would talk too much!"

"What are you saying? You're out of your mind," said Leamas, and his voice held the trace of fear.

"It all held together, you see. Mundt escaped so easily from England; you told me yourself he did. And what did Guillam say to you? He said they didn't *want* to catch him! Why not? I'll tell you why—he was their man; they turned him, they caught him, don't you see, and that was the price of his freedom—that and the money he was paid."

"I tell you you're out of your mind!" Leamas hissed. "He'll kill you if he ever thinks you make up this kind of stuff. It's sugar candy, Fiedler. Shut up and drive us home." At last the hot grip on Leamas' arm relaxed.

"That's where you're wrong. You provided the answer, you yourself, Leamas. That's why we need one another."

"It's not true!" Leamas shouted. "I've told you again and again, they couldn't have done it. The Circus couldn't have run him against the Zone without my knowing! It just wasn't an administrative possibility. You're trying to tell me Control was personally directing the deputy head of the Abteilung without the knowledge of the Berlin station. You're mad, Fiedler, you're just bloody well off your head!" Suddenly he began to laugh quietly. "You may want his job, you poor bastard; that's not unheard of, you know. But this kind of thing went out with bustles." For a moment neither spoke.

"That money," Fiedler said, "in Copenhagen. The bank, replied to your letter. The manager is very worried lest there has been a mistake. The money was drawn by your co-signatory exactly one week after you paid it in. The date it was drawn coincides with a two-day visit which Mundt paid to Denmark in February. He went there under an alias to meet an American agent we have who was attending a world scientists' conference." Fiedler hesitated, then added, "I suppose you ought to write to the bank and tell them everything is quite in order?"

✠ ✠ 15 ✠ Come to the Ball

Liz looked at the letter from Party Centre and wondered what it was about. She found it a little puzzling. She had to admit she was pleased, but why hadn't they consulted her first? Had the District Committee put up her name, or was it Centre's own choice? But no one in Centre knew her, so far as she was aware. She'd met odd speakers of course, and at District Congress she'd shaken hands with the Party Organizer. Perhaps that man from Cultural Relations had remembered her—that fair, rather effeminate man who was so ingratiating. Ashe, that was his name. He'd taken a bit of interest in her and she supposed he might have handed her name on, or remembered her when the Scholarship came up. An odd man, he was; took her to the Black and White for coffee after the meeting and asked her about her boy friends. He hadn't been amorous or anything—she'd thought he was a bit queer, to be honest—but he asked her masses of questions about herself. How long had she been in the Party, did she get homesick living away from her parents? Had she lots of boy friends or was there a special one she carried a torch for? She hadn't cared for him much but his talk had gone down quite well —the worker-state in the German Democratic Republic, the concept of the worker-poet and all that stuff. He certainly knew all about eastern Europe, he must have traveled a lot. She'd guessed he was a schoolmaster, he had that rather didactic, fluent way with him. They'd had a collection for the Fighting Fund afterwards, and Ashe had put a pound in; she'd been absolutely amazed. That was it, she was sure now: it was Ashe who'd remembered her. He'd told someone at London District, and District had told Centre or something like that. It still seemed a funny way to go about things, but then the Party always was secretive—it was part of being a revolutionary party, she supposed. It didn't appeal to Liz much, the secrecy, it seemed dishonest. But she supposed it was necessary, and heaven knows, there were plenty who got a kick out of it.

She read the letter again. It was on Centre's writing paper, with the thick red print at the top and it began "Dear Comrade." It sounded so military to Liz, and she hated that; she'd never quite got used to "Comrade."

DEAR COMRADE,

We have recently had discussions with our Comrades in the Socialist Unity Party of the German Democratic Republic on the possibility of effecting exchanges between party members over here and our comrades in democratic Germany. The idea is to create a basis of exchange at the rank and file level between our two parties. The S.U.P. is aware that the existing discriminatory measures by the British Home Office make it unlikely that their own delegates will be able to come to the United Kingdom in the immediate future, but they feel that an exchange of experiences is all the more important for this reason. They have generously invited us to select five Branch Secretaries with good experience and a good record of stimulating mass action at street level. Each selected comrade will spend three weeks attending Branch discussions, studying progress in industry and social welfare and seeing at first hand the evidence of fascist provocation by the West. This is a grand opportunity for our comrades to profit from the experiences of a young socialist system.

We therefore asked District to put forward the names of young Cadre workers from your areas who might get the biggest advantage from the trip, and your name has been put forward. We want you to go if you possibly can, and carry out the second part of the scheme—which is to establish contact with a Party Branch in the GDR whose members are from similar industrial backgrounds and have the same kind of problems as your own. The Bayswater South Branch has been paired with Neuenhagen, a suburb of Leipzig. Freda Lüman, Secretary of the Neuenhagen branch, is preparing a big welcome. We are sure you are just the Comrade for the job, and that it will be a terrific success. All expenses will be paid by the GDR Cultural Office.

We are sure you realize what a big honor this is, and are confident you will not allow personal considerations to prevent you from accepting. The visits are due to take place at the end of next month, about the 23rd, but the selected Comrades will travel separately as their invitations are not all concurrent. Will you please let us know as soon as possible whether you can accept, and we will let you have further details.

The more she read it, the odder it seemed. Such short notice for a start—how could they know she could get away from the library? Then to her surprise she recalled that Ashe had asked her what she did for her holidays, whether she had taken her leave this year, and whether she had to give a lot of notice if she wanted to claim free time. Why hadn't they told her who the other nominees were? There was no particular reason why they should, perhaps, but it somehow looked odd when they didn't. It was such a *long* letter, too. They were so hard up for secretarial help at Centre they usually kept their letters short, or asked Comrades to ring up. This was so efficient, so well typed, it might not have been done at Centre at all. But it *was* signed by the Cultural Organizer; it was his signature all right, no doubt of that. She'd seen it at the bottom of notices masses of times. And the letter had that awkward, semibureaucratic, semi-Messianic style she had grown accustomed to without ever liking. It was stupid to say she had a good record of stimulating mass action at street level. She hadn't. As a matter of fact she hated that side of party work—the loudspeakers at the factory gates, selling the *Daily* at the street corner, going from door to door at the local elections. Peace work she didn't mind so much, it meant something to her, it made sense. You could look at the kids in the street as you went by, at the mothers pushing their prams and the old people standing in doorways, and you could say, "I'm doing it for them." That really *was* fighting for peace.

But she never quite saw the fighting for votes and the fighting for sales in the same way. Perhaps that was because it cut them down to size, she thought. It was easy when there were a dozen or so together at a Branch meeting to rebuild the world, march at the vanguard of socialism and talk of the inevitability of history. But afterwards she'd go out into the streets with an armful of *Daily Worker*'s, often waiting an hour, two hours, to sell a copy. Sometimes she'd cheat, as the others cheated, and pay for a dozen herself just to get out of it and go home. At the next meeting they'd boast about it—forgetting they'd bought them themselves—"Comrade Gold sold eighteen copies on Saturday night—eighteen!" It would go in the Minutes then, and the Branch bulletin as well. District would rub their hands, and perhaps she'd get a mention in that little panel on the front page about the Fighting Fund. It was such a little world, and she wished they could be more honest. But she lied to herself about it all, too. Perhaps they all did. Or perhaps the others understood more *why* you had to lie so much.

It seemed so odd they'd made her Branch Secretary. It was Mulligan who'd proposed it—"Our young, vigorous *and* attractive comrade. . . ." He'd thought she'd sleep with him if he got her made Secretary. The others had voted for her because they liked her, and because she could type. Because she'd do the work and not try and make them go canvassing on weekends. Not too often anyway. They'd voted for her because they wanted a decent little club, nice and revolutionary and no fuss. It was all such a fraud. Alec had seemed to understand that; he just hadn't taken it seriously. "Some people keep canaries, some people join the Party," he'd said once, and it was true. In Bayswater South it was true anyway, and District knew that perfectly well. That's why it was so peculiar that she had been nominated; that was why she was extremely reluctant to believe that District had even had a hand in it. The explanation, she was sure, was Ashe. Perhaps he had a crush on her; perhaps he wasn't queer but just looked it.

Liz gave a rather exaggerated shrug, the kind of over-stressed gesture people make when they are excited and alone. It was abroad anyway, it was free and it sounded interesting. She had never been abroad, and she certainly couldn't afford the fare herself. It would be rather fun. She had reservations about Germans, that was true. She knew, she had been told, that West Germany was militarist and *revanchist,* and that East Germany was democratic and peace loving. But she doubted whether all the good Germans were on one side and all the bad ones on the other. And it was the bad ones who had killed her father. Perhaps that was why the Party had chosen her—as a generous act of reconciliation. Perhaps that was what Ashe had had in mind when he asked her all those questions. Of course—that was the explanation. She was suddenly filled with a feeling of warmth and gratitude toward the Party. They really were decent people and she was proud and thankful to belong. She went to the desk and opened the drawer where, in an old school satchel, she kept the Branch stationery and the dues stamps. Putting a sheet of paper into her old Underwood typewriter—they'd sent it down from District when they heard she could type; it jumped a bit but otherwise was fine—she typed a neat, grateful letter of acceptance. Centre was such a wonderful thing—stern, benevolent, impersonal, perpetual. They were good, good people. People who fought for peace. As she closed the drawer she caught sight of Smiley's card.

She remembered that little man with the earnest, puckered face, standing at the doorway of her room and saying, "Did the Party know about you and Alec?" How silly she was. Well, this would take her mind off it.

✠ ✠ 16 ✠ Arrest

Fiedler and Leamas drove back the rest of the way in silence. In the dusk the hills were black and cavernous, the pinpoint lights struggling against the gathering darkness like the lights of distant ships at sea.

Fiedler parked the car in a shed at the side of the house and they walked together to the front door. They were about to enter the lodge when they heard a shout from the direction of the trees, followed by someone calling Fiedler's name. They turned, and Leamas distinguished in the twilight twenty yards away three men standing, apparently waiting for Fiedler.

"What do you want?" Fiedler called.

"We want to talk to you. We're from Berlin."

Fiedler hesitated. "Where's that damn guard?" Fiedler asked Leamas. "There should be a guard on the front door."

Leamas shrugged.

"Why aren't the lights on in the hall?" he asked again;

then, still unconvinced, he began walking slowly toward the men.

Leamas waited a moment, then, hearing nothing, made his way through the unlit house to the annex behind it. This was a shoddy barrack hut attached to the back of the building and hidden from all sides by close plantations of young pine trees. The hut was divided into three adjoining bedrooms; there was no corridor. The center room had been given to Leamas, and the room nearest to the main building was occupied by two guards. Leamas never knew who occupied the third. He had once tried to open the connecting door between it and his own room, but it was locked. He had only discovered it was a bedroom by peering through a narrow gap in the lace curtains early one morning as he went for a walk. The two guards, who followed him everywhere at fifty yards' distance, had not rounded the corner of the hut, and he looked in at the window. The room contained a single bed, made, and a small writing desk with papers on it. He supposed that someone, with what passes for German thoroughness, watched him from that bedroom. But Leamas was too old a dog to allow himself to be bothered by surveillance. In Berlin it had been a fact of life—if you couldn't spot it, so much the worse: it only meant they were taking greater care, or you were losing your grip. Usually, because he was good at that kind of thing, because he was observant and had an accurate memory—because, in short, he was good at his job—he spotted them anyway. He knew the formations favored by a shadowing team, he knew the tricks, the weaknesses, the momentary lapses that could give them away. It meant nothing to Leamas that he was watched, but as he walked through the improvised doorway from the lodge to the hut and stood in the guards' bedroom, he had the distinct feeling that something was wrong.

The lights in the annex were controlled from some central point. They were put on and off by an unseen hand. In the mornings he was often awakened by the sudden blaze of the single overhead light in his room. At night he would be hastened to bed by perfunctory darkness. It was only nine o'clock as he entered the annex, and the lights were already out. Usually they stayed on till eleven, but now they were out and the shutters had been lowered. He had left the connecting door from the house open, so that the pale twilight from the hallway reached, but scarcely penetrated, the guards' bedroom, and by it he could just see the two empty beds. As he stood there peering into the room, surprised to find it empty, the door behind him closed. Perhaps by itself, but Leamas made no attempt to open it. It was pitch-dark. No sound accompanied the closing of the door, no click nor footstep. To Leamas, his instinct suddenly alert, it was as if the sound track had stopped. Then he smelled the cigar smoke. It must have been hanging in the air but he had not noticed it till now. Like a blind man, his senses of touch and smell were sharpened by the darkness.

There were matches in his pocket but he did not use them. He took one pace sideways, pressed his back against the wall and remained motionless. To Leamas there could only be one explanation—they were waiting for him to pass from the guards' room to his own and therefore he determined to remain where he was. Then from the direction of the main building whence he had come he heard clearly the sound of a footstep. The door which had just closed was tested, the lock turned and made fast. Still Leamas did not move. Not yet. There was no pretense: he was a prisoner in the hut.

Very slowly, Leamas now lowered himself into a crouch, putting his hand in the side pocket of his jacket as he did so. He was quite calm, almost relieved at the prospect of action, but memories were racing through his mind. "You've nearly always got a weapon: an ashtray, a couple of coins, a fountain pen—anything that will gouge or cut." It was the favorite dictum of the mild little Welsh sergeant at that house near Oxford in the war: "Never use both hands at once, not with a knife, a stick or a pistol; keep your left arm free, and hold it across the belly. If you can't find anything to hit with, keep the hands open and the thumbs stiff." Taking the box of matches in his right hand, he clasped it longways and deliberately crushed it, so that the small, jagged edges of boxwood protruded from between his fingers. This done, he edged his way along the wall until he came to a chair which he knew was in the corner of the room. Indifferent now to the noise he made, he shoved the chair into the center of the floor. Counting his footsteps as he moved back from the chair, he positioned himself in the angle of the two walls. As he did so, he heard the door of his own bedroom flung open. Vainly he tried to discern the figure that must be standing in the doorway, but there was no light from his own room either. The darkness was impenetrable. He dared not move forward to attack, for the chair was now in the middle of the room; it was his tactical advantage, for he knew where it was, and they did not. They must come for him, they must; he could not let them wait until their helper outside had reached the master switch and put on the lights.

"Come on, you windy bastards," he hissed in German. "I'm here, in the corner. Come and get me, can't you?" Not a move, not a sound.

"I'm here, can't you see me? What's the matter then? What's the matter, children, come on, can't you?"

And then he heard one stepping forward, and another following; and then the oath of a man as he stumbled against the chair, and that was the sign that Leamas was waiting for. Tossing away the box of matches he slowly, cautiously crept forward, pace by pace, his left arm extended in the attitude of a man warding off twigs in a wood until, quite gently, he had touched an arm and felt the warm prickly cloth of a military uniform. Still with his left hand Leamas deliberately tapped the arm twice—two distinct taps—and heard a frightened voice whisper close to his ear in German:

"Hans, is it you?"

"Shut up, you fool," Leamas whispered in reply, and in that same moment reached out and grasped the man's hair, pulling his head forward and down, then in a terrible cutting blow drove the side of his right hand into the nape of the neck, pulled him up again by the arm, hit him in the throat with an upward thrust of his open fist, then released him to fall where the force of gravity took him. As the man's body hit the ground, the lights went on.

In the doorway stood a young captain of the People's Police smoking a cigar, and behind him two men. One was in civilian clothes, quite young. He held a pistol in his hand. Leamas thought it was the Czech kind with a loading lever on the spine of the butt. They were all looking at the man on the floor. Somebody unlocked the outer door and Leamas turned to see who it was. As he turned, there was a shout—Leamas thought it was the captain—telling him to stand still. Slowly he turned back and faced the three men.

His hands were still at his side as the blow came. It seemed to crush his skull. As he fell, drifting warmly into unconsciousness, he wondered whether he had been hit with a revolver, the old kind with a swivel on the butt where you fastened the lanvard.

He was wakened by the lag singing and the warder yelling at him to shut up. He opened his eyes and like a brilliant light the pain burst upon his brain. He lay quite still, refusing to close them, watching the sharp, colored fragments racing across his vision. He tried to take stock of himself: his feet were icy cold and he was aware of the sour stench of prison denims. The singing had stopped and suddenly Leamas longed for it to start again, although he knew it never would. He tried to raise his hand and touch the blood that was caked on his cheek, but his hands were behind him, locked together. His feet too must be bound: the blood had left them, that was why they were cold. Painfully he looked about him, trying to lift his head an inch or two from the floor. To his surprise he saw his own knees in front of him. Instinctively he tried to stretch his legs and as he did so his whole body was seized with a pain so sudden and terrible that he screamed out a sobbing agonized cry of self-pity, like the last cry of a man upon the rack. He lay there panting, attempting to master the pain, then through the sheer perversity of his nature he tried again, quite slowly, to straighten his legs. At once the agony returned, but Leamas had found the cause: his hands and feet were chained together behind his back. As soon as he attempted to stretch his legs the chain tightened, forcing his shoulders down and his damaged head onto the stone floor. They must have beaten him up while he was unconscious, his whole body was stiff and bruised and his groin ached. He wondered if he'd killed the guard. He hoped so.

Above him shone the light, large, clinical and fierce. No furniture, just whitewashed walls, quite close all around, and the gray steel door, a smart charcoal gray, the color you see on clever London houses. There was nothing else. Nothing at all. Nothing to think about, just the savage pain.

He must have lain there hours before they came. It grew hot from the light; he was thirsty but he refused to call out. At last the door opened and Mundt stood there. He knew it was Mundt from the eyes. Smiley had told him about them.

✠ ✠ 17 ✠ Mundt

They untied him and let him try to stand. For a moment he almost succeeded, then, as the circulation returned to his hands and feet, and as the joints of his body were released from the contraction to which they had been subject, he fell. They let him lie there, watching him with the detachment of children looking at an insect. One of the guards pushed past Mundt and yelled at Leamas to get up. Leamas crawled to the wall and put the palms of his throbbing hands against the white brick. He was halfway up when the guard kicked him and he fell again. He tried once more and this time the guard let him stand with his back against the wall. He saw the guard move his weight onto his left leg and he knew he would kick him again. With all his remaining strength Leamas thrust himself forward, driving his lowered head into the guard's face. They fell together, Leamas on top. The guard got up and Leamas lay there waiting for the payoff. But Mundt said something to the guard and Leamas felt himself being picked up by the shoulders and feet and heard the door of his cell close as they carried him down the corridor. He was terribly thirsty.

They took him to a small comfortable room, decently furnished with a desk and armchairs. Swedish blinds half covered the barred windows. Mundt sat at the desk and Leamas in an armchair, his eyes half closed. The guards stood at the door.

"Give me a drink," said Leamas.

"Whisky?"

"Water."

Mundt filled a carafe from a basin in the corner, and put it on the table beside him with a glass.

"Bring him something to eat," he ordered, and one of the guards left the room, returning with a mug of soup and some sliced sausage. He drank and ate, and they watched him in silence.

"Where's Fiedler?" Leamas asked finally.

"Under arrest," Mundt replied curtly.

"What for?"

"Conspiring to sabotage the security of the people."

Leamas nodded slowly. "So you won," he said. "When did you arrest him?"

"Last night."

Leamas waited a moment, trying to focus again on Mundt. "What about me?" he asked.

"You're a material witness. You will of course stand trial yourself later."

"So I'm part of a put-up job by London to frame Mundt, am I?"

Mundt nodded, lit a cigarette and gave it to one of the sentries to pass to Leamas. "That's right," he said. The sentry came over, and with a gesture of grudging solicitude, put the cigarette between Leamas' lips.

"A pretty elaborate operation," Leamas observed, and added stupidly, "Clever chaps these Chinese."

Mundt said nothing. Leamas became used to his silences as the interview progressed. Mundt had rather a pleasant voice, that was something Leamas hadn't expected, but he seldom spoke. It was part of Mundt's extraordinary self-confidence, perhaps, that he did not speak unless he specifically wished to, that he was prepared to allow long silences to intervene rather than exchange pointless words. In this he differed from professional interrogators who set store by initiative, by the evocation of atmosphere and the exploitation of that psychological dependency of a prisoner upon his inquisitor. Mundt despised technique: he was a man of fact and action. Leamas preferred that.

Mundt's appearance was fully consistent with his temperament. He looked an athlete. His fair hair was cut short. It lay mat and neat. His young face had a hard, clean line, and a frightening directness; it was barren of humor or fantasy. He looked young but not youthful; older men would take him seriously. He was well built. His clothes fitted him because he was an easy man to fit. Leamas found no difficulty in recalling that Mundt was a killer. There was a coldness about him, a rigorous self-sufficiency which perfectly equipped him for the business of murder. Mundt was a very hard man.

"The other charge on which you will stand trial, if necessary," Mundt added quietly, "is murder."

"So the sentry died, did he?" Leamas replied.

A wave of intense pain passed through his head.

Mundt nodded. "That being so," he said, "your trial for espionage is somewhat academic. I propose that the case against Fiedler should be publicly heard. That is also the wish of the Praesidium."

"And you want my confession?"

"Yes."

"In other words you haven't any proof."

"We shall have proof. We shall have your confession." There was no menace in Mundt's voice. There was no style, no theatrical twist. "On the other hand, there could be mitigation in your case. You were blackmailed by British Intelligence; they accused you of stealing money and then coerced you into preparing a *revanchist* trap against myself. The court would have sympathy for such a plea."

Leamas seemed to be taken off his guard.

"How did you know they accused me of stealing money?" But Mundt made no reply.

"Fiedler has been very stupid," Mundt observed. "As soon as I read the report of our friend Peters I knew why you had been sent, and I knew that Fiedler would fall into the trap. Fiedler hates me so much." Mundt nodded, as if to emphasize the truth of his observation. "Your people knew that of course. It was a very clever operation. Who prepared it, tell me. Was it Smiley? Did he do it?" Leamas said nothing.

"I wanted to see Fiedler's report of his own interrogation of you, you see. I told him to send it to me. He procrastinated and I knew I was right. Then yesterday he circulated it among the Praesidium, and did not send me a copy. Someone in London has been very clever."

Leamas said nothing.

"When did you last see Smiley?" Mundt asked casually. Leamas hesitated, uncertain of himself. His head was aching terribly.

"When did you last see him?" Mundt repeated.

"I don't remember," Leamas said at last; "he wasn't really in the outfit any more. He'd drop in from time to time."

"He is a great friend of Peter Guillam, is he not?"

"I think so, yes."

"Guillam, you thought, studied the economic situation in the GDR. Some odd little section in your Service; you weren't quite sure what it did."

"Yes." Sound and sight were becoming confused in the mad throbbing of his brain. His eyes were hot and painful. He felt sick.

"Well, when did you last see Smiley?"

"I don't remember . . . I don't remember."

Mundt shook his head.

"You have a very good memory—for anything that incriminates me. We can all remember when we *last* saw somebody. Did you, for instance, see him after you returned from Berlin?"

"Yes, I think so. I bumped into him . . . in the Circus once, in London." Leamas had closed his eyes and he was sweating. "I can't go on, Mundt . . . not much longer, Mundt . . . I'm sick," he said.

"After Ashe had picked you up, after he had walked into the trap that had been set for him, you had lunch together, didn't you?"

"Yes. Lunch together."

"Lunch ended at about four o'clock. Where did you go then?"

"I went down to the City, I think. I don't remember for sure . . . For Christ's sake, Mundt," he said holding his head with his hand, "I can't go on. My bloody head's . . ."

"And after that where did you go? Why did you shake off your followers, why were you so keen to shake them off?"

Leamas said nothing: he was breathing in sharp gasps, his head buried in his hands.

"Answer this one question, then you can go. You shall have a bed. You can sleep if you want. Otherwise you must go back to your cell, do you understand? You will be tied up again and fed on the floor like an animal, do you understand? Tell me where you went."

The wild pulsation of his brain suddenly increased, the room was dancing; he heard voices around him and the sound of footsteps; spectral shapes passed and repassed, detached from sound and gravity; someone was shouting, but not at him; the door was open, he was sure someone had opened the door. The room was full of people, all shouting now, and then they were going, some of them had gone, he heard them marching away, the stamping of their feet was like the throbbing of his head; the echo died and there was silence. Then like the touch of mercy itself, a cool cloth was laid across his forehead, and kindly hands carried him away.

He woke on a hospital bed, and standing at the foot of it was Fiedler, smoking a cigarette.

✠ ✠ 18 ✠ Fiedler

Leamas took stock. A bed with sheets. A single ward with no bars in the windows, just curtains and frosted glass. Pale green walls, dark green linoleum; and Fiedler watching him, smoking.

A nurse brought him food: an egg, some thin soup and fruit. He felt like death, but he supposed he'd better eat it. So he did and Fiedler watched.

"How do you feel?" he asked.

"Bloody awful," Leamas replied.

"But better?"

"I suppose so." He hesitated. "Those sods beat me up."

"You killed a sentry, you know that?"

"I guessed I had. . . . What do they expect if they mount such a damn stupid operation? Why didn't they pull us both in at once? Why put all the lights out? If anything was over-organized, that was."

"I am afraid that as a nation we tend to overorganize. Abroad that passes for efficiency."

180

Again there was a pause.

"What happened to you?" Leamas asked.

"Oh, I too was softened for interrogation."

"By Mundt's men?"

"By Mundt's men *and* Mundt. It was a very peculiar sensation!"

"That's one way of putting it."

"No, no; not physically. Physically it was a nightmare, but you see Mundt had a special interest in beating me up. Apart from the confession."

"Because you dreamed up that story about—"

"Because I am a Jew."

"Oh Christ," said Leamas softly.

"That is why I got special treatment. All the time he whispered to me. It was very strange."

"What did he say?"

Fiedler didn't reply. At last he muttered, "That's all over."

"Why? What's happened?"

"The day we were arrested I had applied to the Praesidium for a civil warrant to arrest Mundt as an enemy of the people."

"But you're mad—I told you, you're raving mad, Fiedler! He'll never—"

"There was other evidence against him apart from yours. Evidence I have been accumulating over the last three years, piece by piece. Yours provided the proof we need; that's all. As soon as that was clear I prepared a report and sent it to every member of the Praesidium except Mundt. They received it on the same day that I made my application for a warrant."

"The day we were pulled in."

"Yes. I knew Mundt would fight. I knew he had friends on the Praesidium, or yes-men at least, people who were sufficiently frightened to go running to him as soon as they got my report. And in the end, I knew he would lose. The Praesidium had the weapon it needed to destroy him; they had the report, and for those few days while you and I were being questioned they read it and reread it until they knew it was true and each knew the others knew. In the end they acted. Herded together by their common fear, their common weakness and their common knowledge, they turned against him and ordered a Tribunal."

"Tribunal?"

"A secret one, of course. It meets tomorrow. Mundt is under arrest."

"What is this other evidence? The evidence you've collected."

"Wait and see," Fiedler replied with a smile. "Tomorrow you will see."

Fiedler was silent for a time, watching Leamas eat.

"This Tribunal," Leamas asked, "how is it conducted?"

"That is up to the President. It is not a People's Court—it is important to remember that. It is more in the nature of an inquiry—a committee of inquiry, that's it, appointed by the Praesidium to investigate and report upon a certain . . . subject. Its report contains a recommendation. In a case like this the recommendation is tantamount to a verdict, but remains secret, as a part of the proceedings of the Praesidium."

"How does it work? Are there counsel and judges?"

"There are three judges," Fiedler said; "and in effect, there are counsel. Tomorrow I myself shall put the case against Mundt. Karden will defend him."

"Who's Karden?"

Fiedler hesitated.

"A very tough man," he said. "Looks like a country doctor, small and benevolent. He was at Buchenwald."

"Why can't Mundt defend himself?"

"It was Mundt's wish. It is said that Karden will call a
witness."

Leamas shrugged. "That's your affair," he said.

Again there was silence. At last Fiedler said reflectively,
"I wouldn't have minded—I don't think I would have
minded, not so much anyway—if he had hurt me for myself,
for hate or jealousy. Do you understand that? That long, long
pain and all the time you say to yourself, 'Either I shall faint
or I shall grow to bear the pain, nature will see to that'
and the pain just increases like a violinist going up the E
string. You think it can't get any higher and it does—the
pain's like that, it rises and rises, and all that nature does is
bring you on from note to note like a deaf child being taught
to hear. And all the time he was whispering Jew . . . Jew.
I could understand, I'm sure I could, if he had done it for the
idea, for the Party if you like, or if he had hated *me*. But it
wasn't that; he hated—"

"All right," said Leamas shortly, "you should know. He's
a bastard."

"Yes," said Fiedler, "he is a bastard." He seemed excited;
he wants to boast to somebody, thought Leamas.

"I thought a lot about you," Fiedler added. "I thought
about that talk we had—you remember—about the motor."

"What motor?"

Fiedler smiled. "I'm sorry, that is a direct translation. I
mean '*Motor*,' the engine, spirit, urge; whatever Christians
call it."

"I'm not a Christian."

Fiedler shrugged. "You know what I mean." He smiled

again. "The thing that embarrasses you. . . . I'll put it another way. Suppose Mundt is right? He asked me to confess, you know; I was to confess that I was in league with British spies who were plotting to murder him. You see the argument—that the whole operation was mounted by British Intelligence in order to entice us—me, if you like—into liquidating the best man in the Abteilung. To turn our own weapon against us."

"He tried that on me," said Leamas indifferently. And he added, "As if I'd cooked up the whole bloody story."

"But what I mean is this: suppose you had done that, suppose it were true—I am taking an example, you understand, a hypothesis, would you kill a man, an innocent man—"

"Mundt's a killer himself."

"Suppose he wasn't. Suppose it were me they wanted to kill: would London do it?"

"It depends. It depends on the need. . . ."

"Ah," said Fiedler contentedly, "it depends on the need. Like Stalin, in fact. The traffic accident and the statistics. That is a great relief."

"Why?"

"You must get some sleep," said Fiedler. "Order what food you want. They will bring you whatever you want. Tomorrow you can talk." As he reached the door he looked back and said, "We're all the same, you know, that's the joke."

Soon Leamas was asleep, content in the knowledge that Fiedler was his ally and that they would shortly send Mundt to his death. That was something which he had looked forward to for a very long time.

⚔ ⚔ 19 ⚔ Branch Meeting

Liz was happy in Leipzig. Austerity pleased her—it gave her the comfort of sacrifice. The little house she stayed in was dark and meager, the food was poor and most of it had to go to the children. They talked politics at every meal, she and Frau Lüman, Branch Secretary for the Ward Branch of Leipzig-Neuenhagen, a small gray woman whose husband managed a gravel quarry on the outskirts of the city. It was like living in a religious community, Liz thought; a convent or a kibbutz or something. You felt the world was better for your empty stomach. Liz had some German which she had learned from her aunt, and she was surprised how quickly she was able to use it. She tried it on the children first and they grinned and helped her. The children treated her oddly to begin with, as if she were a person of great quality or rarity value, and on the third day one of them plucked up courage and asked her if she had brought any chocolate from *"drüben"*—from "over there." She'd never thought of that and she felt ashamed. After that they seemed to forget about her.

In the evenings there was Party work. They distributed literature, visited Branch members who had defaulted on their dues or lagged behind in their attendance at meetings, called in at District for a discussion on "Problems Connected with the Centralized Distribution of Agricultural Produce" at which all local Branch Secretaries were present, and attended a meeting of the Workers' Consultative Council of a machine tool factory on the outskirts of the town.

At last, on the fourth day, a Thursday, came their own Branch Meeting. This was to be, for Liz at least, the most exhilarating experience of all; it would be an example of all that her own Branch in Bayswater could one day be. They had chosen a wonderful title for the evening's discussions—"Coexistence After Two Wars"—and they expected a record attendance. The whole ward had been circularized; they had taken care to see that there was no rival meeting in the neighborhood that evening; it was not a late shopping day.

Seven people came.

Seven people and Liz and the Branch Secretary and the man from District. Liz put a brave face on it but she was terribly upset. She could scarcely concentrate on the speaker, and when she tried he used long German compounds that she couldn't work out anyway. It was like the meetings in Bayswater, it was like midweek evensong when she used to go to church—the same dutiful little group of lost faces, the same fussy self-consciousness, the same feeling of a great idea in the hands of little people. She always felt the same thing—it was awful really but she did—she wished no one would turn up, because that was absolute and it suggested persecution, humiliation—it was something you could react to.

But seven people were nothing: they were worse than nothing, because they were evidence of the inertia of the uncapturable mass. They broke your heart.

The room was better than the schoolroom in Bayswater, but even that was no comfort. In Bayswater it had been fun trying to *find* a room. In the early days they had pretended they were something else, not the Party at all. They'd taken back rooms in pubs, a committee room at the Ardena Café, or met secretly in one another's houses. Then Bill Hazel had joined from the Secondary School and they'd used his classroom. Even that was a risk—the headmaster thought Bill ran a drama group, so theoretically at least they might still be chucked out. Somehow that fitted better than this Peace Hall in pre-cast concrete with the cracks in the corners and the picture of Lenin. Why did they have that silly frame thing all around the picture? Bundles of organ pipes sprouting from the corners and the bunting all dusty. It looked like something from a fascist funeral. Sometimes she thought Alec was right—you believed in things because you needed to; what you believed in had no value of its own, no function. What did he say? "A dog scratches where it itches. Different dogs itch in different places." No, it was wrong, Alec was wrong —it was a wicked thing to say. Peace and freedom and equality—they were facts, of course they were. And what about history—all those laws the Party proved? No, Alec was wrong: truth existed outside people, it was demonstrated in history, individuals must bow to it, be crushed by it if necessary. The Party was the vanguard of history, the spearpoint in the fight for Peace . . . She went over the rubric a little uncertainly. She wished more people had come. Seven was so few. They looked so cross; cross and hungry.

The meeting over, Liz waited for Frau Lüman to collect the unsold literature from the heavy table by the door, fill in

her attendance book and put on her coat, for it was cold that
evening. The speaker had left—rather rudely, Liz thought—
before the general discussion. Frau Lüman was standing at
the door with her hand on the light switch when a man
appeared out of the darkness, framed in the doorway. Just for
a moment Liz thought it was Ashe. He was tall and fair and
wore one of those raincoats with leather buttons.

"Comrade Lüman?" he inquired.

"Yes?"

"I am looking for an English Comrade, Gold. She is staying with you?"

"I'm Elizabeth Gold," Liz put in, and the man came into
the hall, closing the door behind him so that the light shone
full upon his face.

"I am Halten from District." He showed some paper to
Frau Lüman who was still standing at the door, and· she
nodded and glanced a little anxiously toward Liz.

"I have been asked to give a message to Comrade Gold
from the Praesidium," he said. "It concerns an alteration in
your program; an invitation to attend a special meeting."

"Oh," said Liz rather stupidly. It seemed fantastic that the
Praesidium should even have heard of her.

"It is a gesture," Halten said. "A gesture of goodwill."

"But I . . . but Frau Lüman . . ." Liz began helplessly.

"Comrade Lüman, I am sure, will forgive you under the
circumstances."

"Of course," said Frau Lüman quickly.

"Where is the meeting to be held?"

"It will necessitate your leaving tonight," Halten replied.
"We have a long way to go. Nearly to Görlitz."

"To Görlitz. . . . Where is that?"

"East," said Frau Lüman quickly. "On the Polish border."

"We can drive you home now. You can collect your things and we will continue the journey at once."

"Tonight? Now?"

"Yes." Halten didn't seem to consider Liz had much choice.

A large black car was waiting for them. There was a driver in the front and a flag post on the hood. It looked like a military car.

✠ ✠ 20 ✠ Tribunal

The court was no larger than a school-room. At one end, on the mere five or six benches which were provided, sat guards and warders and here and there among them spectators—members of the Praesidium and selected officials. At the other end of the room sat the three members of the Tribunal on tall-backed chairs at an unpolished oak table. Above them, suspended from the ceiling by three loops of wire, was a large red star made of plywood. The walls of the courtroom were white like the walls of Leamas' cell.

On either side, their chairs a little forward of the table and turned inwards to face one another, sat two men: one was middle-aged, sixty perhaps, in a black suit and a gray tie, the kind of suit they wear in church in German country districts; the other was Fiedler.

Leamas sat at the back, a guard on either side of him. Between the heads of the spectators he could see Mundt, himself surrounded by police, his fair hair cut very short, his broad shoulders covered in the familiar gray of prison uniform. It seemed to Leamas a curious commentary on the mood of the court—or the influence of Fiedler—that he himself should be wearing his own clothes, while Mundt was in prison uniform.

Leamas had not long been in his place when the President of the Tribunal, sitting at the center of the table, rang the bell. The sound directed his attention toward it, and a shiver passed over him as he realized that the President was a woman. He could scarcely be blamed for not noticing it before. She was fiftyish, small-eyed and dark. Her hair was cut short like a man's, and she wore the kind of functional dark tunic favored by Soviet wives. She looked sharply around the room, nodded to a sentry to close the door, and began at once without ceremony to address the court.

"You all know why we are here. The proceedings are secret, remember that. This is a Tribunal convened expressly by the Praesidium. It is to the Praesidium alone that we are responsible. We shall hear evidence as we think fit." She pointed perfunctorily toward Fiedler. "Comrade Fiedler, you had better begin."

Fiedler stood up. Nodding briefly toward the table, he drew from the briefcase beside him a sheaf of papers held together in one corner by a piece of black cord.

He talked quietly and easily, with a diffidence which Leamas had never seen in him before. Leamas considered it a good performance, well adjusted to the role of a man regretfully hanging his superior.

"You should know first, if you do not know already," Fiedler began, "that on the day that the Praesidium received my report on the activities of Comrade Mundt I was arrested, together with the defector Leamas. Both of us were imprisoned and both of us . . . invited, under extreme duress, to confess that this whole terrible charge was a fascist plot against a loyal Comrade.

"You can see from the report I have already given you how it was that Leamas came to our notice: we ourselves sought him out, induced him to defect and finally brought him to Democratic Germany. Nothing could more clearly demonstrate the impartiality of Leamas than this: that he still refuses, for reasons I will explain, to believe that Mundt was a British agent. It is therefore grotesque to suggest that Leamas is a plant: the initiative was ours, and the fragmentary but vital evidence of Leamas provides only the final proof in a long chain of indications reaching back over the last three years.

"You have before you the written record of this case. I need do no more than interpret for you facts of which you are already aware.

"The charge against Comrade Mundt is that he is the agent of an imperialist power. I could have made other charges—that he passed information to the British Secret Service, that he turned his Department into the unconscious lackey of 'a bourgeois state, that he deliberately shielded *revanchist* anti-Party groups and accepted sums of foreign currency in reward. These other charges would derive from the first; that Hans-Dieter Mundt is the agent of an imperialist power. The penalty for this crime is death. There is no crime more serious in our penal code, none which exposes our state to greater danger, nor demands more vigilance of our Party organs." Here he put the papers down.

"Comrade Mundt is forty-two years old. He is Deputy Head of the Department for the Protection of the People. He is unmarried. He has always been regarded as a man of exceptional capabilities, tireless in serving the Party's interests, ruthless in protecting them.

"Let me tell you some details of his career. He was recruited into the Department at the age of twenty-eight and underwent the customary instruction. Having completed his probationary period he undertook special tasks in Scandinavian countries—notably Norway, Sweden and Finland—where he succeeded in establishing an intelligence network which carried the battle against fascist agitators into the enemy's camp. He performed this task well, and there is no reason to suppose that at that time he was other than a diligent member of his Department. But, Comrades, you should not forget this early connection with Scandinavia. The networks established by Comrade Mundt soon after the war provided the excuse, many years later, for him to travel to Finland and Norway, where his commitments became a cover enabling him to draw thousands of dollars from foreign banks in return for his treacherous conduct. Make no mistake: Comrade Mundt has not fallen victim to those who try to disprove the arguments of history. First cowardice, then weakness, then greed were his motives; the acquirement of great wealth his dream. Ironically, it was the elaborate system by which his lust for money was satisfied that brought the forces of justice on his trail."

Fiedler paused, and looked around the room, his eyes suddenly alight with fervor. Leamas watched, fascinated.

"Let that be a lesson," Fiedler shouted, "to those other enemies of the state, whose crime is so foul that they must plot in the secret hours of the night!" A dutiful murmur rose from the tiny group of spectators at the back of the room.

"They will not escape the vigilance of the people whose

blood they seek to sell!" Fiedler might have been addressing a large crowd rather than the handful of officials and guards assembled in the tiny, white-walled room.

Leamas realized at that moment that Fiedler was taking no chances: the deportment of the Tribunal, prosecutors and witnesses must be politically impeccable. Fiedler, knowing no doubt that the danger of a subsequent countercharge was inherent in such cases, was protecting his own back: the polemic would go down in the record and it would be a brave man who set himself to refute it.

Fiedler now opened the file that lay on the desk before him.

"At the end of 1956, Mundt was posted to London as a member of the East German Steel Mission. He had the additional special task of undertaking countersubversionary measures against *émigré* groups. In the course of his work he exposed himself to great dangers—of that there is no doubt—and he obtained valuable results."

Leamas' attention was again drawn to the three figures at the center table. To the President's left, a youngish man, dark. His eyes seemed to be half closed. He had lank, unruly hair and the gray, meager complexion of an ascetic. His hands were slim, restlessly toying with the corner of a bundle of papers which lay before him. Leamas guessed he was Mundt's man; he found it hard to say why. On the other side of the table sat a slightly older man, balding, with an open agreeable face. Leamas thought he looked rather an ass. He guessed that if Mundt's fate hung in the balance, the young man would defend him and the woman condemn. He thought the second man would be embarrassed by the difference of opinion and side with the President.

Fiedler was speaking again.

"It was at the end of his service in London that recruitment took place. I have said that he exposed himself to great dangers; in doing so he fell foul of the British Secret Police, and they issued a warrant for his arrest. Mundt, who had no diplomatic immunity (NATO Britain does not recognize our sovereignty), went into hiding. Ports were watched; his photograph and description were distributed throughout the British Isles. Yet after two days in hiding, Comrade Mundt took a taxi to London airport and flew to Berlin. 'Brilliant,' you will say, and so it was. With the whole of Britain's police force alerted, her roads, railways, shipping and air routes under constant surveillance, Comrade Mundt takes a plane from London airport. Brilliant indeed. Or perhaps you may feel, Comrades, with the advantage of hindsight, that Mundt's escape from England was a little *too* brilliant, a little *too* easy, that without the connivance of the British authorities it would never have been possible at all!" Another murmur, more spontaneous than the first, rose from the back of the room.

"The truth is this: Mundt *was* taken prisoner by the British; in a short historic interview they offered him the classic alternative. Was it to be years in an imperialist prison, the end of a brilliant career, or was Mundt to make a dramatic return to his home country, against all expectation, and fulfill the promise he had shown? The British, of course, made it a condition of his return that he should provide them with information, and they would pay him large sums of money. With the carrot in front and the stick behind, Mundt was recruited.

"It was now in the British interest to promote Mundt's career. We cannot yet prove that Mundt's success in liquidating minor Western intelligence agents was the work of his imperialist masters betraying their own collaborators—those who were expendable—in order that Mundt's prestige should be enhanced. We cannot prove it, but it is an assumption which the evidence permits.

"Ever since 1960—the year Comrade Mundt became head of the Counterespionage Section of the Abteilung—indications have reached us from all over the world that there was a highly placed spy in our ranks. You all know Karl Riemeck was a spy; we thought when he was eliminated that the evil had been stamped out. But the rumors persisted.

"In late 1960 a former collaborator of ours approached an Englishman in the Lebanon known to be in contact with their Intelligence Service. He offered him—we found out soon afterwards—a complete breakdown of the two sections of the Abteilung for which he had formerly worked. His offer, after it had been transmitted to London, was rejected. That was a very curious thing. It could only mean that the British already possessed the intelligence they were being offered, *and that it was up to date.*

"From mid-1960 onwards we were losing collaborators abroad at an alarming rate. Often they were arrested within a few weeks of their dispatch. Sometimes the enemy attempted to turn our own agents back on us, but not often. It was as if they could scarcely be bothered.

"And then—it was early 1961 if my memory is correct— we had a stroke of luck. We obtained by means I will not describe a summary of the information which British Intelligence held about the Abteilung. It was complete, it was accurate, and it was astonishingly up to date. I showed it to Mundt, of course—he was my superior. He told me it came as no surprise to him: he had certain inquiries in hand and I should take no action for fear of prejudicing them. And I confess that at that moment the thought crossed my mind, remote and fantastic as it was, that Mundt himself could have provided the information. There were other indications too. . . .

"I need hardly tell you that the last, the very last person to be suspected of espionage is the head of the Counterespionage Section. The notion is so appalling, so melodramatic, that few would entertain it, let alone give expression to it! I confess that I myself have been guilty of excessive reluctance in reaching such a seemingly fantastic deduction. That was erroneous.

"But, Comrades, the final evidence has been delivered into our hands. I propose to call that evidence now." He turned, glancing toward the back of the room. "Bring Leamas forward."

The guards on either side of him stood up and Leamas edged his way along the row to the rough gangway which ran not more than two feet wide, down the middle of the room. A guard indicated to him that he should stand facing the table. Fiedler stood a bare six feet away from him. First the President addressed him.

"Witness, what is your name?" she asked.

"Alec Leamas."

"What is your age?"

"Fifty."

"Are you married?"

"No."

"But you were."

"I'm not married now."

"What is your profession?"

"Assistant librarian."

Fiedler angrily intervened. "You were formerly employed by British Intelligence, were you not?" he snapped.

"That's right. Till a year ago."

"The Tribunal has read the reports of your interrogation," Fiedler continued. "I want you to tell them again about the conversation you had with Peter Guillam sometime in May last year."

"You mean when we talked about Mundt?"

"Yes."

"I've told you. It was at the Circus, the office in London, our headquarters in Cambridge Circus. I bumped into Peter in the corridor. I knew he was mixed up with the Fennan Case and I asked him what had become of George Smiley. Then we got to talking about Dieter Frey, who died, and Mundt, who was mixed up in the thing. Peter said he thought that Maston—Maston was effectively in charge of the case then—had not wanted Mundt to be caught."

"How did you interpret that?" asked Fiedler.

"I knew Maston had made a mess of the Fennan Case. I supposed he didn't want any mud raked up by Mundt appearing at the Old Bailey."

"If Mundt had been caught, would he have been legally charged?" the President put in.

"It depends on who caught him. If the police got him they'd report it to the Home Office. After that no power on earth could stop him from being charged."

"And what if your Service had caught him?" Fiedler inquired.

"Oh, that's a different matter. I suppose they would either have interrogated him and then tried to exchange him for one of our own people in prison over here; or else they'd have given him a ticket."

"What does that mean?"

"Got rid of him."

"Liquidated him?" Fiedler was asking all the questions now, and the members of the Tribunal were writing diligently in the files before them.

"I don't know what they do. I've never been mixed up in that game."

"Might they not have tried to recruit him as their agent?"

"Yes, but they didn't succeed."

"How do you know that?"

"Oh, for God's sake, I've told you over and over again. I'm not a bloody performing seal! I was head of the Berlin Command for four years. If Mundt had been one of our people, I would have known. I couldn't have helped knowing."

"Quite."

Fiedler seemed content with that answer, confident perhaps that the remainder of the Tribunal was not. He now turned his attention to Operation "Rolling Stone," took Leamas once again through the special security complexities governing the circulation of the file, the letters to the Stockholm and Helsinki banks and the one reply which Leamas had received. Addressing himself to the Tribunal, Fiedler commented:

"We had no reply from Helsinki. I do not know why. But let me recapitulate for you. Leamas deposited money at Stockholm on June fifteenth. Among the papers before you there is the facsimile of a letter from the Royal Scandinavian Bank addressed to Robert Lang. Robert Lang was the name Leamas used to open the Copenhagen deposit account. From that letter (it is the twelfth serial in your files) you will see that the entire sum—ten thousand dollars—was drawn by the cosignatory to the account one week later. I imagine," Fiedler continued, indicating with his head the motionless figure of Mundt in the front row, "that it is not disputed by the defendant that he was in Copenhagen on June twenty-first, nominally engaged on secret work on behalf of the Abteilung." He paused and then continued:

"Leamas' visit to Helsinki—the second visit he made to deposit money—took place on about September twenty-fourth." Raising his voice, he turned and looked directly at Mundt. "On the third of October Comrade Mundt made a clandestine journey to Finland—once more allegedly in the interests of the Abteilung."

There was silence. Fiedler turned slowly and addressed himself once more to the Tribunal. In a voice at once subdued and threatening he asked, "Are you complaining that the evidence is circumstantial? Let me remind you of something more." He turned to Leamas.

"Witness, during your activities in Berlin you became associated with Karl Riemeck, formerly Secretary to the Praesidium of the Socialist Unity Party. What was the nature of that association?"

"He was my agent until he was shot by Mundt's men."

"Quite so. He was shot by Mundt's men. One of several spies who were summarily liquidated by Comrade Mundt before they could be questioned. But before he was shot by Mundt's men he was an agent of the British Secret Service?"

Leamas nodded.

"Will you describe Riemeck's meeting with the man you call Control."

"Control came over to Berlin from London to see Karl. Karl was one of the most productive agents we had, I think, and Control wanted to meet him."

Fiedler put in: "He was also one of the most trusted?"

"Yes, oh yes. London loved Karl, he could do no wrong. When Control came out I fixed it for Karl to come to my flat and the three of us dined together. I didn't like Karl's coming there really, but I couldn't tell Control that. It's hard to explain, but they get ideas in London, they're so cut off from it and I was frightened stiff they'd find some excuse for taking over Karl themselves—they're quite capable of it."

"So you arranged for the three of you to meet," Fiedler put in curtly. "What happened?"

"Control asked me beforehand to see that he had a quarter of an hour alone with Karl, so during the evening I pretended to have run out of Scotch. I left the flat and went over to de Jong's place. I had a couple of drinks there, borrowed a bottle and came back."

"How did you find them?"

"What do you mean?"

"Were Control and Riemeck talking still? If so, what were they talking about?"

"They weren't talking at all when I came back."

"Thank you. You may sit down."

Leamas returned to his seat at the back of the room. Fiedler turned to the three members of the Tribunal and began:

"I want to talk first about the spy Riemeck, who was shot —Karl Riemeck. You have before you a list of all the information which Riemeck passed to Alec Leamas in Berlin, so far as Leamas can recall it. It is a formidable record of treachery. Let me summarize it for you. Riemeck gave to his masters a detailed breakdown of the work and personalities of the whole Abteilung. He was able, if Leamas is to be believed, to describe the workings of our most secret sessions. As secretary to the Praesidium he gave minutes of its most secret proceedings.

"That was easy for him; he himself compiled the record of every meeting. But Riemeck's *access* to the secret affairs of the Abteilung is a different matter. Who at the end of 1959 co-opted Riemeck onto the Committee for the Protection of the People, that vital subcommittee of the Praesidium which coordinates and discusses the affairs of our security organs? Who proposed that Riemeck should have the privilege of access to the files of the Abteilung? Who at every stage in Riemeck's career *since* 1959 (the year Mundt returned from England, you remember) singled him out for posts of exceptional responsibility? I will tell you," Fiedler proclaimed. "The same man who was uniquely placed to shield him in his espionage activities: Hans-Dieter Mundt. Let us recall how Riemeck contacted the Western Intelligence Agencies in Berlin—how he sought out de Jong's car on a picnic and put the film inside it. Are you not amazed at Riemeck's foreknowledge? How could he have known where to find that car, and on that very day? Riemeck had no car himself, he could not have followed de Jong from his house in West Berlin. There was only one way he could have known—through the agency of our own Security Police, who reported de Jong's presence as a matter of routine as soon as the car passed the Inter Sector checkpoint. That knowledge was available to Mundt, and Mundt made it available to Riemeck. *That* is the case against Hans-Dieter Mundt—I tell you, Riemeck was his creature, the link between Mundt and his imperialist masters!"

Fiedler paused, then added quietly, "Mundt—Riemeck—Leamas: that was the chain of command, and it is axiomatic of intelligence technique the whole world over that each link of the chain be kept, as far as possible, in ignorance of the others. Thus it is *right* that Leamas should maintain he knows nothing to the detriment of Mundt: that is no more than the proof of good security by his masters in London.

"You have also been told how the whole case known as 'Rolling Stone' was conducted under conditions of special secrecy, how Leamas knew in vague terms of an intelligence section under Peter Guillam which was supposedly concerned with economic conditions in our Republic—a section which surprisingly was on the distribution list of 'Rolling Stone.' Let me remind you that that same Peter Guillam was one of several British Security officers who were involved in the investigation of Mundt's activities while he was in England."

The youngish man at the table lifted his pencil, and looking at Fiedler with his hard, cold eyes wide open he asked, "Then why did Mundt liquidate Riemeck, if Riemeck was his agent?"

"He had no alternative. Riemeck was under suspicion. His mistress had betrayed him by boastful indiscretion. Mundt gave the order that he be shot on sight, got word to Riemeck to run, and the danger of betrayal was eliminated. Later, Mundt assassinated the woman.

"I want to speculate for a moment on Mundt's technique. After his return to Germany in 1959, British Intelligence played a waiting game. Mundt's willingness to cooperate with them had yet to be demonstrated, so they gave him instructions and waited, content to pay their money and hope for the best. At that time Mundt was not a senior functionary of our Service—nor of our Party—but he saw a good deal, and what he saw he began to report. He was, of course, communicating with his masters unaided. We must suppose that he was met in West Berlin, that on his short journeys abroad to Scandinavia and elsewhere he was contacted and interrogated. The British must have been wary to begin with— who would not be? They weighed what he gave them with painful care against what they already knew, but they feared that he would play a double game. But gradually they realized they had hit a gold mine. Mundt took to his treacherous work with the systematic efficiency for which he is renowned.

At first—this is my guess, but it is based, Comrades, on long experience of this work and on the evidence of Leamas— for the first few months they did not dare to establish any kind of network which included Mundt. They let him be a lone wolf, they serviced him, paid and instructed him independently of their Berlin organization. They established in London, under Guillam (for it was he who recruited Mundt in England), a tiny undercover section whose function was not known even within the Service save to a select circle. They paid Mundt by a special system which they called Rolling Stone, and no doubt they treated the information he gave them with prodigious caution. Thus, you see, it is consistent with Leamas' protestations that the existence of Mundt was unknown to him although—as you will see—he not only paid him, but in the end *actually received from Riemeck and passed to London the intelligence which Mundt obtained.*

"Toward the end of 1959, Mundt informed his London masters that he had found within the Praesidium a man who would act as intermediary between them and Mundt. That man was Karl Riemeck.

"How did Mundt find Riemeck? How did he dare to establish Riemeck's willingness to cooperate? You must remember Mundt's exceptional position: he had access to all the security files, could tap telephones, open letters, employ watchers; he could interrogate anyone with undisputed right, and had before him the detailed picture of their private life. Above all he could silence suspicion in a moment by turning against the people the very weapon"—Fiedler's voice was trembling with fury—"which was designed for their protection." Returning effortlessly to his former rational style, he continued:

"You can see now what London did. Still keeping Mundt's identity a close secret, they connived at Riemeck's enlistment and enabled indirect contact to be established between

Mundt and the Berlin command. That is the significance of Riemeck's contact with de Jong and Leamas. *That* is how you should interpret Leamas' evidence, *that* is how you should measure Mundt's treachery."

He turned and, looking Mundt full in the face, he shouted: "There is your saboteur, terrorist! There is the man who has sold the people's right!

"I have nearly finished. Only one more thing needs to be said. Mundt gained a reputation as a loyal and astute protector of the people, and he silenced forever those tongues that could betray his secret. Thus he killed in the name of the people to protect his fascist treachery and advance his own career within our Service. It is not possible to imagine a crime more terrible than this. That is why—in the end—having done what he could to protect Karl Riemeck from the suspicion which was gradually surrounding him, he gave the order that Riemeck be shot on sight. That is why he arranged for the assassination of Riemeck's mistress. When you come to give your judgment to the Praesidium, do not shrink from recognizing the full bestiality of this man's crime. For Hans-Dieter Mundt, death is a judgment of mercy."

⚔ ⚔ 21 ⚔ The Witness

The President turned to the little man in the black suit sitting directly opposite Fiedler.

"Comrade Karden, you are speaking for Comrade Mundt. Do you wish to examine the witness Leamas?"

"Yes, yes, I should like to in one moment," he replied, getting laboriously to his feet and pulling the ends of his gold-rimmed spectacles over his ears. He was a benign figure, a little rustic, and his hair was white.

"The contention of Comrade Mundt," he began—his mild voice was rather pleasantly modulated—"is that Leamas is lying; that Comrade Fiedler either by design or ill chance has been drawn into a plot to disrupt the Abteilung, and thus bring into disrepute the organs for the defense of our socialist state. We do not dispute that Karl Riemeck was a British spy—there is evidence for that. But we dispute that Mundt was in league with him, or accepted money for betraying our Party. We say there is no objective evidence for this charge, that Comrade Fiedler is intoxicated by dreams of power and blinded to rational thought. We maintain that from the moment Leamas returned from Berlin to London he lived a part; that he simulated a swift decline into degeneracy, drunkenness and debt, that he assaulted a tradesman in full public view and affected anti-American sentiments—all solely in order to attract the attention of the Abteilung. We believe that British Intelligence has deliberately spun around Comrade Mundt a mesh of circumstantial evidence—the payment of money to foreign banks, its withdrawal to coincide with Mundt's presence in this or that country, the casual hearsay evidence from Peter Guillam, the secret meeting between Control and Riemeck at which matters were discussed that Leamas could not hear: these all provided a spurious chain of evidence and Comrade Fiedler, on whose ambitions the British so accurately counted, accepted it; and thus he became party to a monstrous plot to destroy—to murder in fact, for Mundt now stands to lose his life—one of the most vigilant defenders of our Republic.

"Is it not consistent with their record of sabotage, subversion and human trafficking that the British should devise this desperate plot? What other course lies open to them now that the rampart has been built across Berlin and the flow of Western spies has been checked? We have fallen victim to their plot; at best Comrade Fiedler is guilty of a most serious error; at worst of conniving with imperialist spies to undermine the security of the worker state, and shed innocent blood.

"We also have a witness." He nodded benignly at the court. "Yes. We too have a witness. For do you really suppose that all this time Comrade Mundt has been in ignorance of Fiedler's fevered plotting? Do you really suppose that? For months he has been aware of the sickness in Fiedler's mind. It was Comrade Mundt himself who authorized the approach that was made to Leamas in England: do you think he would have taken such an insane risk if he were himself to be implicated?

"And when the reports of Leamas' first interrogation in The Hague reached the Praesidium, do you suppose Comrade Mundt threw his away unread? And when, after Leamas had arrived in our country and Fiedler embarked on his own interrogation, no further reports were forthcoming, do you suppose Comrade Mundt was then so obtuse that he did not know what Fiedler was hatching? When the first reports came in f. ɔm Peters in The Hague, Mundt had only to look at the dates of Leamas' visits to Copenhagen and Helsinki to realize that the whole thing was a plant—a plant to discredit Mundt himself. Those dates did indeed coincide with Mundt's visits to Denmark and Finland: they were chosen by London for that very reason. Mundt had known of those 'earlier indications' as well as Fiedler—remember that. Mundt too was looking for a spy within the ranks of the Abteilung. . . .

"And so by the time Leamas arrived in Democratic Germany, Mundt was watching with fascination how Leamas nourished Fiedler's suspicions with hints and oblique indications—never overdone, you understand, never emphasized, but dropped here and there with perfidious subtlety. And by then the ground had been prepared—the man in the Lebanon, the miraculous scoop to which Fiedler referred, both seeming to confirm the presence of a highly placed spy within the Abteilung. . . .

"It was wonderfully well done. It could have turned—it could still turn—the defeat which the British suffered through the loss of Karl Riemeck into a remarkable victory.

"Comrade Mundt took one precaution while the British,

with Fiedler's aid, planned his murder. He caused scrupulous inquiries to be made in London. He examined every tiny detail of that double life which Leamas led in Bayswater. He was looking, you see, for some human error in a scheme of almost superhuman subtlety. Somewhere, he thought, in Leamas' long sojourn in the wilderness he would have to break faith with his oath of poverty, drunkenness, degeneracy, above all of solitude. He would need a companion, a mistress perhaps; he would long for the warmth of human contact, long to reveal a part of the other soul within his breast. Comrade Mundt was right, you see. Leamas, that skilled, experienced operator, made a mistake so elementary, so human that—" He smiled. "You shall hear the witness, but not yet. The witness is here; procured by Comrade Mundt. It was an admirable precaution. Later I shall call—that witness." He looked a trifle arch, as if to say he must be allowed his little joke. "Meanwhile I should like, if I may, to put one or two questions to this reluctant incriminator, Mr. Alec Leamas."

"Tell me," he began, "are you a man of means?"

"Don't be bloody silly," said Leamas shortly. "You know how I was picked up."

"Yes, indeed," Karden declared, "it was masterly. I may take it, then, that you have no money at all?"

"You may."

"Have you friends who would lend you money, give it to you perhaps? Pay your debts?"

"If I had I wouldn't be here now."

"You have none? You cannot imagine that some kindly

benefactor, someone perhaps you have almost forgotten about, would ever concern himself with putting you on your feet . . . settling with creditors and that kind of thing?"

"No."

"Thank you. Another question: do you know George Smiley?"

"Of course I do. He was in the Circus."

"He has now left British Intelligence?"

"He packed it up after the Fennan Case."

"Ah yes—the case in which Mundt was involved. Have you ever seen him since?"

"Once or twice."

"Have you seen him since you left the Circus?"

Leamas hesitated. "No," he said.

"He didn't visit you in prison?"

"No. No one did."

"And before you went to prison?"

"No."

"After you left prison—the day of your release, in fact—you were picked up, weren't you, by a man called Ashe?"

"Yes."

"You had lunch with him in Soho. After the two of you had parted, where did you go?"

"I don't remember. Probably I went to a pub. No idea."

"Let me help you. You went to Fleet Street eventually and caught a bus. From there you seem to have zigzagged by bus, tube and private car—rather inexpertly for a man of your experience—to Chelsea. Do you remember that? I can show you the report if you like, I have it here."

"You're probably right. So what?"

"George Smiley lives in Bywater Street, just off the King's Road, that is my point. Your car turned into Bywater Street and our agent reported that you were dropped at number nine. That happens to be Smiley's house."

"That's drivel," Leamas declared. "I should think I went to the Eight Bells; it's a favorite pub of mine."

"By private car?"

"That's nonsense too. I went by taxi, I expect. If I have money I spend it."

"But why all the running about beforehand?"

"That's just cock. They were probably following the wrong man. That would be bloody typical."

"Going back to my original question, you cannot imagine that Smiley would have taken any interest in you after you left the Circus?"

"God, no."

"Nor in your welfare after you went to prison, nor spent money on your dependents, nor wanted to see you after you had met Ashe?"

"No. I haven't the least idea what you're trying to say, Karden, but the answer's no. If you'd ever met Smiley you wouldn't ask. We're about as different as we could be."

Karden seemed rather pleased with this, smiling and nodding to himself as he adjusted his spectacles and referred elaborately to his file.

"Oh yes," he said, as if he had forgotten something, "when you asked the grocer for credit, how much money had you?"

"Nothing," said Leamas carelessly. "I'd been broke for a week. Longer, I should think."

"What had you lived on?"

"Bits and pieces. I'd been ill—some fever. I'd hardly eaten anything for a week. I suppose that made me nervous too—tipped the scales."

"You were, of course, still owed money at the library, weren't you?"

"How did you know that?" asked Leamas sharply. "Have you been—"

"Why didn't you go and collect it? Then you wouldn't have had to ask for credit, would you, Leamas?"

He shrugged.

"I forget. Probably because the library was closed on Saturday mornings."

"I see. Are you sure it was closed on Saturday mornings?"

"No. It's just a guess."

"Quite. Thank you, that is all I have to ask."

Leamas was sitting down as the door opened and a woman came in. She was large and ugly, wearing a gray overall with chevrons on one sleeve. Behind her stood Liz.

✠ ✠ 22 ✠ The President

She entered the court slowly, looking around her, wide-eyed, like a half-awakened child entering a brightly lit room. Leamas had forgotten how young she was. When she saw him sitting between two guards, she stopped.

"Alec."

The guard beside her put his hand on her arm and guided her forward to the spot where Leamas had stood. It was very quiet in the courtroom.

"What is your name, child?" the President asked abruptly. Liz's long hands hung at her sides, the fingers straight.

"What is your name?" she repeated, loudly this time.

"Elizabeth Gold."

"You are a member of the British Communist Party?"

"Yes."

"And you have been staying in Leipzig?"

"Yes."

"When did you join the Party?"

"Nineteen fifty-five. No—fifty-four, I think it was—"

She was interrupted by the sound of movement; the screech of furniture forced aside, and Leamas' voice, hoarse, high-pitched, ugly, filling the room.

"You bastards! Leave her alone!"

Liz turned in terror and saw him standing, his white face bleeding and his clothes awry, saw a guard hit him with his fist, so that he half fell; then they were both upon him, had lifted him up, thrusting his arms high behind his back. His head fell forward on his chest, then jerked sideways in pain.

"If he moves again, take him out," the President ordered, and she nodded to Leamas in warning, adding: "You can speak again later if you want. Wait." Turning to Liz she said sharply, "Surely you know when you joined the Party?"

Liz said nothing, and after waiting a moment the President shrugged. Then leaning forward and staring at Liz intently she asked:

"Elizabeth, have you ever been told in your Party about the need for secrecy?"

Liz nodded.

"And you have been told never, never to ask questions of another Comrade on the organization dispositions of the Party?"

Liz nodded again. "Yes," she said, "of course."

"Today you will be severely tested in that rule. It is better for you, far better, that you should know nothing. Nothing," she added with sudden emphasis. "Let this be enough: we three at this table hold very high rank in the Party. We are acting with the knowledge of our Praesidium, in the interests of Party security. We have to ask you some questions, and your answers are of the greatest importance. By replying truthfully and bravely you will help the cause of socialism."

"But *who*," she whispered, "*who* is on trial? What's Alec done?"

The President looked past her at Mundt and said, "Perhaps no one is on trial. That is the point. Perhaps only the accusers. It can make no difference *who* is accused," she added, "it is a guarantee of your impartiality that you cannot know."

Silence descended for a moment on the little room; and then, in a voice so quiet that the President instinctively turned her head to catch her words, she asked, "Is it Alec? Is it Leamas?"

"I tell you," the President insisted, "it is better for you—far better—you should not know. You must tell the truth and go. That is the wisest thing you can do."

Liz must have made some sign or whispered some words the others could not catch, for the President again leaned forward and said, with great intensity, "Listen, child, do you want to go home? Do as I tell you and you shall. But if you—" She broke off, indicated Karden with her hand and added cryptically, "This Comrade wants to ask you some questions, not many. Then you shall go. Tell the truth."

Karden stood again, and smiled his kindly, churchwarden smile.

"Elizabeth," he inquired, "Alec Leamas was your lover, wasn't he?"

She nodded.

"You met at the library in Bayswater, where you work."

"Yes."

"You had not met him before?"

She shook her head. "We met at the library," she said.

"Have you had many lovers, Elizabeth?"

Whatever she said was lost as Leamas shouted again,

"Karden, you swine," but as she heard him she turned and said, quite loud, "Alec, don't. They'll take you away."

"Yes," observed the President drily; "they will."

"Tell me," Karden resumed smoothly, "was Alec a Communist?"

"No."

"Did he know you were a Communist?"

"Yes. I told him."

"What did he say when you told him then, Elizabeth?"

She didn't know whether to lie, that was the terrible thing. The questions came so quickly she had no chance to think. All the time they were listening, watching, waiting for a word, a gesture perhaps, that could do terrible harm to Alec. She couldn't lie unless she knew what was at stake; she would fumble on and Alec would die—for there was no doubt in her mind that Leamas was in danger.

"What did he say then?" Karden repeated.

"He laughed. He was above all that kind of thing."

"Do you believe he was above it?"

"Of course."

The young man at the Judges' table spoke for the second time. His eyes were half closed:

"Do you regard that as a valid judgment of a human being? That he is *above* the course of history and the compulsions of dialectic?"

"I don't know. It's what I believed, that's all."

"Never mind," said Karden. "Tell me, was he a *happy* person, always laughing and that kind of thing?"

"No. He didn't often laugh."

"But he laughed when you told him you were in the Party. Do you know why?"

"I think he despised the Party."

"Do you think he *hated* it?" Karden asked casually.

"I don't know," Liz replied pathetically.

"Was he a man of strong likes and dislikes?"

"No . . . no; he wasn't."

"But he assaulted a grocer. Now why did he do that?"

Liz suddenly didn't trust Karden any more. She didn't trust the caressing voice and the good-fairy face.

"I don't know."

"But you thought about it?"

"Yes."

"Well, what conclusion did you come to?"

"None," said Liz flatly.

Karden looked at her thoughtfully, a little disappointed perhaps, as if she had forgotten her catechism.

"Did you," he asked—it might have been the most obvious of questions—"did you *know* that Leamas was going to hit the grocer?"

"No," Liz replied, perhaps too quickly, so that in the pause that followed Karden's smile gave way to a look of amused curiosity.

"Until now, until today," he asked finally, "when had you last seen Leamas?"

"I didn't see him again after he went to prison," Liz replied.

"When did you see him last, then?" The voice was kind but persistent.

Liz hated having her back to the court; she wished she could turn and see Leamas, see his face perhaps; read in it some guidance, some sign telling how to answer. She was becoming frightened for herself; these questions which proceeded from charges and suspicions of which she knew nothing. They must know she wanted to help Alec, that she was afraid, but no one helped her—why would no one help her?

"Elizabeth, when was your last meeting with Leamas until today?" Oh that voice, how she hated it, that silken voice.

"The night before it happened," she replied, "the night before he had the fight with Mr. Ford."

"The fight? It wasn't a fight, Elizabeth. The grocer never hit back, did he—he never had a chance. Very unsporting!" Karden laughed, and it was all the more terrible because no one laughed with him. "Tell me, where did you meet Leamas that last night?"

"At his flat. He'd been ill, not working. He'd been in bed and I'd been coming in and cooking for him."

"And buying the food? Shopping for him?"

"Yes."

"How kind. It must have cost you a lot of money," Karden observed sympathetically. "Could you afford to keep him?"

"I didn't keep him. I got it from Alec. He—"

"Oh," said Karden sharply, "so he *did* have some money?"

Oh God, thought Liz, oh God, oh dear God, what have I said?

"Not much," she said quickly, "not much, I know. A pound, two pounds, not more. He didn't have more than that. He couldn't pay his bills—his electric light and his rent—they were all paid afterwards, you see, after he'd gone, by a friend. A friend had to pay, not Alec."

"Of course," said Karden quietly, "a friend paid. Came specially and paid all his bills. Some old friend of Leamas, someone he knew before he came to Bayswater, perhaps. Did you ever meet this friend, Elizabeth?"

She shook her head.

"I see. What other bills did this good friend pay, do you know?"

"No . . . no."

"Why do you hesitate?"

"I said I don't know," Liz retorted fiercely.

"But you hesitated," Karden explained. "I wondered if you had second thoughts."

"No."

"Did Leamas ever speak of this friend? A friend with money who knew where Leamas lived?"

"He never mentioned a friend at all. I didn't think he had any friends."

"Ah."

There was a terrible silence in the courtroom, more terrible to Liz because like a blind child among the seeing she was cut off from all those around her; they could measure her answers against some secret standard, and she could not know from the dreadful silence what they had found.

"How much money do you earn, Elizabeth?"

"Six pounds a week."

"Have you any savings?"

"A little. A few pounds."

"How much is the rent of your flat?"

"Fifty shillings a week."

"That's quite a lot, isn't it, Elizabeth? Have you paid your rent recently?"

She shook her head helplessly.

"Why not?" Karden continued. "Have you no money?"

In a whisper she replied: "I've got a lease. Someone bought the lease and sent it to me."

"Who?"

"I don't know." Tears were running down her face. "I don't know. . . . Please don't ask any more questions. I don't know who it was . . . six weeks ago they sent it, a bank in the City . . . some Charity had done it . . . a thousand pounds. I swear I don't know who . . . a gift from a Charity, they said. You know everything . . . you tell me who . . ."

Burying her face in her hands she wept, her back still

turned to the court, her shoulders moving as the sobs shook her body. No one moved, and at length she lowered her hands but did not look up.

"Why didn't you inquire?" Karden asked simply. "Or are you used to receiving anonymous gifts of a thousand pounds?"

She said nothing and Karden continued: "You didn't inquire because you guessed. Isn't that right?"

Raising her hand to her face again, she nodded.

"You guessed it came from Leamas, or from Leamas' friend, didn't you?"

"Yes," she managed to say. "I heard in the Street that the grocer had got some money, a lot of money from somewhere after the trial. There was a lot of talk about it, and I knew it must be Alec's friend. . . ."

"How very strange," said Karden almost to himself. "How odd." And then: "Tell me, Elizabeth, did anyone get in touch with you after Leamas went to prison?"

"No," she lied. She knew now, she was sure they wanted to prove something against Alec, something about the money or his friends; something about the grocer.

"Are you sure?" Karden asked, his eyebrows raised above the gold rims of his spectacles.

"Yes."

"But your neighbor, Elizabeth," Karden objected patiently, "says that men called—two men—quite soon after Leamas had been sentenced; or were they just lovers, Elizabeth? Casual lovers, like Leamas, who gave you money?"

"Alec *wasn't* a casual lover!" she cried. "How can you—"

"But he gave you money. Did the men give you money, too?"

"Oh God," she sobbed, "don't ask—"

"Who were they?" She did not reply, then Karden shouted,

quite suddenly; it was the first time he had raised his voice. "Who?"

"I don't know. They came in a car. Friends of Alec."

"More friends? What did they want?"

"I don't know. They kept asking me what he had told me. They told me to get in touch with them if—"

"How? How get in touch with them?"

At last she replied: "He lived in Chelsea . . . his name was Smiley . . . George Smiley . . . I was to ring him."

"And did you?"

"No!"

Karden had put down his file. A deathly silence had descended on the court. Pointing toward Leamas, Karden said, in a voice more impressive because it was perfectly under control:

"Smiley wanted to know whether Leamas had told her too much. Leamas had done the one thing British Intelligence had never expected him to do: he had taken a girl and wept on her shoulder."

Then Karden laughed quietly, as if it were all such a neat joke. "Just as Karl Riemeck did. He's made the same mistake."

"Did Leamas ever talk about himself?" Karden continued.

"No."

"You know nothing about his past?"

"No. I knew he'd done something in Berlin. Something for the Government."

"Then he did talk about his past, didn't he? Did he tell you he had been married?"

There was a long silence. Liz nodded.

"Why didn't you see him after he went to prison? You could have visited him."

"I didn't think he'd want me to."

"I see. Did you write to him?"

"No. Yes, once . . . just to tell him I'd wait. I didn't think he'd mind."

"You didn't think he would want that either?"

"No."

"And when he had served his time in prison, you didn't try to get in touch with him?"

"No."

"Did he have anywhere to go, did he have a job waiting for him—friends who would take him in?"

"I don't know . . . I don't know."

"In fact, you were finished with him, weren't you?" Karden asked with a sneer. "Had you found another lover?"

"No! I waited for him . . . I'll always wait for him." She checked herself. "I wanted him to come back."

"Then why had you not written? Why didn't you try to find out where he was?"

"He didn't want me to, don't you see! He made me promise . . . never to follow him . . . never to . . ."

"*So he expected to go to prison, did he?*" Karden demanded triumphantly.

"No—I don't know. How can I tell you what I don't know?"

"And on that last evening," Karden persisted, his voice harsh and bullying, "on the evening before he hit the grocer, did he make you renew your promise? Well, did he?"

With infinite weariness, she nodded in a pathetic gesture of capitulation. "Yes."

"And you said good-bye?"

"We said good-bye."

"After supper, of course. It was quite late. Or did you spend the night with him?"

"After supper. I went home—not straight home. I went for a walk first, I don't know where. Just walking."

"What reason did he give for breaking off your relationship?"

"He didn't break it off," she said. "Never. He just said there was something he had to do; someone he had to get even with, whatever it cost, and afterwards, one day perhaps, when it was all over . . . he would . . . come back, if I was still there and . . ."

"And you said," Karden suggested with irony, "that you would always wait for him, no doubt? That you would always love him?"

"Yes," Liz replied simply.

"Did he say he would send you money?"

"He said . . . he said things weren't as bad as they seemed. That I would be . . . looked after."

"And that was why you didn't inquire, afterwards, wasn't it, when some Charity in the City casually gave you a thousand pounds?"

"Yes! Yes, that's right! Now you know everything—you knew it all already. Why did you send for me if you knew?"

Imperturbably Karden waited for her sobbing to stop.

"That," he observed finally to the Tribunal before him, "is the evidence of the defense. I am sorry that a girl whose perception is clouded by sentiment and whose alertness is blunted by money should be considered by our British comrades a suitable person for Party office."

Looking first at Leamas and then at Fiedler he added brutally: "She is a fool. It is fortunate, nevertheless, that Leamas met her. This is not the first time that a *revanchist* plot has been uncovered through the decadence of its architects."

With a little, precise bow toward the Tribunal, Karden sat down.

As he did so, Leamas rose to his feet, and this time the guards let him alone.

London must have gone raving mad. He'd told them—that was the joke—he'd told them to leave her alone. And now it was clear that from the moment, the very moment he left England—before that, even, as soon as he went to prison—some bloody fool had gone round tidying up—paying the bills, settling the grocer, the landlord; above all, Liz. It was insane, fantastic. What were they trying to do—kill Fiedler, kill their agent? Sabotage their own operation? Was it just Smiley? Had his wretched little conscience driven him to this? There was only one thing to do—get Liz and Fiedler out of it and carry the can. He was probably written off anyway. If he could save Fiedler's skin—if he could do that—perhaps there was a chance that Liz would get away.

How the hell did they know so much? He was sure he hadn't been followed to Smiley's house that afternoon. And the money—how did they pick up the story about him stealing money from the Circus? That was designed for internal consumption only . . . then how? For God's sake, how?

Bewildered, angry and bitterly ashamed, he walked slowly up the gangway, stiffly, like a man going to the scaffold.

✠ ✠ **23** ✠ **Confession**

"All right, Karden." His face was white and hard as stone, his head tilted back, a little to one side, in the attitude of a man listening to some distant sound. There was a frightful stillness about him, not of resignation but of self-control, so that his whole body seemed to be in the iron grip of his will.

"All right, Karden, let her go."

Liz was staring at him, her face crumpled and ugly, her dark eyes filled with tears.

"No, Alec . . . no," she said. There was no one else in the room—just Leamas tall and straight like a soldier.

"Don't tell them," she said, her voice rising, "whatever it is, don't tell them just because of me. . . . I don't mind any more, Alec. I promise I don't."

"Shut up, Liz," said Leamas awkwardly. "It's too late now." His eyes turned to the President. "She knows nothing. Nothing at all. Get her out of here and send her home. I'll tell you the rest."

The President glanced briefly at the men on either side of her. She deliberated, then said, "She can leave the court, but she cannot go home until the hearing is finished. Then we shall see."

"She knows nothing, I tell you!" Leamas shouted. "Karden's right, don't you see? It was an operation, a planned operation. How could she know that? She's just a frustrated little girl from a crackpot library—she's no good to you!"

"She is a witness," replied the President shortly. "Fiedler may want to question her." It wasn't Comrade Fiedler any more.

At the mention of his name, Fiedler seemed to wake from the reverie into which he had sunk, and Liz looked at him consciously for the first time. His deep brown eyes rested on her for a moment, and he smiled very slightly, as if in recognition of her race. He was a small, forlorn figure, oddly relaxed she thought.

"She knows nothing," Fiedler said. "Leamas is right, let her go." His voice was tired.

"You realize what you are saying?" the President asked. "You realize what this means? Have *you* no questions to put to her?"

"She has said what she had to say." Fiedler's hands were folded on his knees and he was studying them as if they interested him more than the proceedings of the court. "It was all most cleverly done." He nodded. "Let her go. She cannot tell us what she does not know." With a certain mock formality he added, "I have no questions for the witness."

A guard unlocked the door and called into the passage outside. In the total silence of the court they heard a woman's answering voice, and her ponderous footsteps slowly approaching. Fiedler abruptly stood up and taking Liz by the arm, he guided her to the door. As she reached the door she turned and looked back toward Leamas but he was staring away from her like a man who cannot bear the sight of blood.

"Go back to England," Fiedler said to her. "You go back to England." Suddenly Liz began to sob uncontrollably. The wardress put an arm around her shoulder, more for support than comfort, and led her from the room. The guard closed the door. The sound of her crying faded gradually to nothing.

"There isn't much to say," Leamas began. "Karden's right. It was a put-up job. When we lost Karl Riemeck we lost our only decent agent in the Zone. All the rest had gone already. We couldn't understand it—Mundt seemed to pick them up almost before we'd recruited them. I came back to London and saw Control. Peter Guillam was there and George Smiley. George was in retirement really, doing something clever. Philology or something.

"Anyway, they'd dreamed up this idea. Set a man to trap himself, that's what Control said. Go through the motions and see if they bite. Then we worked it out—backwards so to speak. 'Inductive' Smiley called it. If Mundt *were* our agent how would we have paid him, how would the files look, and so on. Peter remembered that some Arab had tried to sell us a breakdown of the Abteilung a year or two back and we'd sent him packing. Afterwards we found out we'd made a mistake. Peter had the idea of fitting that in—as if we'd turned it down because we already knew. That was clever.

"You can imagine the rest. The pretense of going to pieces; drink, money troubles, the rumors that Leamas had robbed the till. It all hung together. We got Elsie in Accounts to help with the gossip, and one or two others. They did it bloody well," he added with a touch of pride. "Then I chose a morning—a Saturday morning, lots of people about—and broke out. It made the local press—it even made the *Worker*, I think—and by that time you people had picked it up. From then on," he added with contempt, "you dug your own graves."

"Your grave," said Mundt quietly. He was looking thoughtfully at Leamas with his pale, pale eyes. "And perhaps Comrade Fiedler's."

"You can hardly blame Fiedler," said Leamas indifferently, "he happened to be the man on the spot; he's not the only man in the Abteilung who'd willingly hang you, Mundt."

"We shall hang you, anyway," said Mundt reassuringly. "You murdered a guard. You tried to murder me."

Leamas smiled drily.

"All cats are alike in the dark, Mundt. . . . Smiley always said it could go wrong. He said it might start a reaction we couldn't stop. His nerve's gone—you know that. He's never been the same since the Fennan Case—since the Mundt affair in London. They say something happened to him then—that's why he left the Circus. That's what I can't make out, why they paid off the bills, the girl and all that. It must have been Smiley wrecking the operation on purpose, it must have been. He must have had a crisis of conscience, thought it was wrong to kill or something. It was mad, after all that preparation, all that work, to mess up an operation that way.

"But Smiley hated you, Mundt. We all did, I think, although we didn't say it. We planned the thing as if it was all a bit of a game . . . it's hard to explain now. We knew we had our backs to the wall: we'd failed against Mundt and now we were going to try to kill him. But it was still a game." Turning to the Tribunal he said: "You're wrong about Fiedler; he's not ours. Why would London take this kind of risk with a man in Fiedler's position? They counted on him, I admit. They knew he hated Mundt—why shouldn't he? Fiedler's a Jew, isn't he? You know, you must know, all of you, what Mundt's reputation is, what he thinks about Jews.

"I'll tell you something—no one else will, so I'll tell you. Mundt had Fiedler beaten up, and all the time, while it was going on, Mundt baited him and jeered at him for being a Jew. You all know what kind of man Mundt is, and you put up with him because he's good at his job. But"—he faltered for a second, then continued—"but for God's sake . . . enough people have got mixed up in all this without Fiedler's head going into the basket. Fiedler's all right, I tell you . . . idealogically sound, that's the expression, isn't it?"

He looked at the Tribunal. They watched him impassively, curiously almost, their eyes steady and cold. Fiedler, who had returned to his chair and was listening with rather studied detachment, looked at Leamas blankly for a moment.

"And you messed it all up, Leamas, is that it?" he asked. "An old dog like Leamas, engaged in the crowning operation of his career, falls for a . . . what did you call her? . . . a frustrated little girl in a crackpot library? London must have known; Smiley couldn't have done it alone." Fiedler turned to Mundt. "Here's an odd thing, Mundt; they must have known you'd check up on every part of his story. That was why Leamas lived the life. Yet afterwards they sent money to the grocer, paid up the rent; and they bought the lease for the girl. Of all the extraordinary things for them to do, people of their experience, to pay a thousand pounds to a girl—*to a member of the Party*—who was supposed to believe he was broke. Don't tell me Smiley's conscience goes that far. London must have done it. What a risk!"

Leamas shrugged.

"Smiley was right. We couldn't stop the reaction. We never expected you to bring me here—Holland, yes—but not here." He fell silent for a moment, then continued. "And I never thought you'd bring the girl. I've been a bloody fool."

"But Mundt hasn't," Fiedler put in quickly. "Mundt knew what to look for—he even knew the girl would provide the proof—very clever of Mundt, I must say. He even knew about that lease—amazing really. I mean, how *could* he have found out? She didn't tell anyone. I know that girl, I understand her . . . she wouldn't tell anyone at all." He glanced toward Mundt. "Perhaps Mundt can tell us how he knew?"

Mundt hesitated, a second too long, Leamas thought.

"It was her subscription," he said. "A month ago she increased her Party contribution by ten shillings a month. I heard about it. And so I tried to establish how she could afford it. I succeeded."

"A masterly explanation," Fiedler replied coolly.

There was silence.

"I think," said the President, glancing at her two colleagues, "that the Tribunal is now in a position to make its report to the Praesidium. That is," she added, turning her small, cruel eyes on Fiedler, "unless you have anything more to say."

Fiedler shook his head. Something still seemed to amuse him.

"In that case," the President continued, "my colleagues are agreed that Comrade Fiedler should be relieved of his duties until the disciplinary committee of the Praesidium has considered his position.

"Leamas is already under arrest. I would remind you all that the Tribunal has no executive powers. The People's Prosecutor, in collaboration with Comrade Mundt, will no doubt consider what action is to be taken against a British *agent provocateur* and murderer."

She glanced past Leamas at Mundt. But Mundt was looking at Fiedler with the dispassionate regard of a hangman measuring his subject for the rope.

And suddenly, with the terrible clarity of a man too long deceived, Leamas understood the whole ghastly trick.

☒ ☒ **24** ☒ **The Commissar**

Liz stood at the window, her back to the wardress, and stared blankly into the tiny yard outside. She supposed the prisoners took their exercise there. She was in somebody's office; there was food on the desk beside the telephones but she couldn't touch it. She felt sick and terribly tired; physically tired. Her legs ached, her face felt stiff and raw from weeping. She felt dirty and longed for a bath.

"Why don't you eat?" the woman asked again. "It's all over now." She said this without compassion, as if the girl were a fool not to eat when the food was there.

"I'm not hungry."

The wardress shrugged. "You may have a long journey," she observed, "and not much at the other end."

"What do you mean?"

"The workers are starving in England," she declared complacently. "The capitalists let them starve."

Liz thought of saying something but there seemed no

point. Besides, she wanted to know; she had to know, and this woman could tell her.

"What is this place?"

"Don't you know?" The wardress laughed. "You should ask them over there." She nodded toward the window. "They can tell you what it is."

"Who are they?"

"Prisoners."

"What kind of prisoners?"

"Enemies of the state," she replied promptly. "Spies, agitators."

"How do you know they are spies?"

"The Party knows. The Party knows more about people than they know themselves. Haven't you been told that?" The wardress looked at her, shook her head and observed, "The English! The rich have eaten your future and your poor have given them the food—that's what's happened to the English."

"Who told you that?"

The woman smiled and said nothing. She seemed pleased with herself.

"And this is a prison for spies?" Liz persisted.

"It is a prison for those who fail to recognize socialist reality; for those who think they have the right to err; for those who slow down the march. Traitors," she concluded briefly.

"But what have they done?"

"We cannot build Communism without doing away with individualism. You cannot plan a great building if some swine builds his sty on your site."

Liz looked at her in astonishment.

"Who told you all this?"

"I am Commissar here," she said proudly. "I work in the prison."

"You are very clever," Liz observed, approaching her.

"I am a worker," the woman replied acidly. "The concept of brain workers as a higher category must be destroyed. There are no categories, only workers; no antithesis between physical and mental labor. Haven't you read Lenin?"

"Then the people in this prison are intellectuals?"

The woman smiled. "Yes," she said, "they are reactionaries who call themselves progressive: they defend the individual against the state. Do you know what Khrushchev said about the counterrevolution in Hungary?"

Liz shook her head. She must show interest, she must make the woman talk.

"He said it would never have happened if a couple of writers had been shot in time."

"Who will they shoot now?" Liz asked quickly. "After the trial?"

"Leamas," she replied indifferently, "and the Jew, Fiedler." Liz thought for a moment she was going to fall but her hand found the back of a chair and she managed to sit down.

"What has Leamas done?" she whispered. The woman looked at her with her small, cunning eyes. She was very large; her hair was scant, stretched over her head to a bun at the nape of her thick neck. Her face was heavy, her complexion flaccid and watery.

"He killed a guard," she said.

"Why?"

The woman shrugged.

"As for the Jew," she continued, "he made an accusation against a loyal comrade."

"Will they shoot Fiedler for that?" asked Liz incredulously.

"Jews are all the same," the woman commented. "Comrade Mundt knows what to do with Jews. We don't need their kind here. If they join the Party they think it belongs to them.

If they stay out, they think it is conspiring against them. It is said that Leamas and Fiedler plotted together against Mundt. Are you going to eat that?" she inquired, indicating the food on the desk. Liz shook her head. "Then I must," she declared, with a grotesque attempt at reluctance. "They have given you a potato. You must have a lover in the kitchen." The humor of this observation sustained her until she had finished the last of Liz's meal.

Liz went back to the window.

In the confusion of Liz's mind, in the turmoil of shame and grief and fear, there predominated the appalling memory of Leamas as she had last seen him in the courtroom, sitting stiffly in his chair, his eyes averted from her own. She had failed him and he dared not look at her before he died; would not let her see the contempt, the fear perhaps, that was written on his face.

But how could she have done otherwise? If Leamas had only told her what he had to do—even now it wasn't clear to her—she would have lied and cheated for him, anything, if he had only told her! Surely he understood that; surely he knew her well enough to realize that in the end she would do whatever he said, that she would take on his form and being, his will, life, his image, his pain, if she could; that she prayed for nothing more than the chance to do so. But how could she have known, if she was not told, how to answer those veiled, insidious questions? There seemed no end to the destruction she had caused. She remembered, in the fevered condition of her mind, how, as a child, she had been horrified to learn that with every step she made, thousands of minute creatures were destroyed beneath her foot; and now, whether she had lied or told the truth—or even, she was sure, had kept silent—she had been forced to destroy a human being; perhaps two, for was there not also the Jew, Fiedler, who had been gentle with her, taken her arm and told her to go back to England? They would shoot Fiedler; that's what the woman said. Why did it have to be Fiedler—why not the old man who asked the questions, or the fair one in the front row between the soldiers, the one who smiled all the time? Whenever she turned around she had caught sight of his smooth, blond head and his smooth, cruel face smiling as if it were all a great joke. It comforted her that Leamas and Fiedler were on the same side.

She turned to the woman again and asked, "Why are we waiting here?"

The wardress pushed the plate aside and stood up.

"For instructions," she replied. "They are deciding whether you must stay."

"Stay?" repeated Liz blankly.

"It is a question of evidence. Fiedler may be tried. I told you: they suspect conspiracy between Fiedler and Leamas."

"But who against? How could he conspire in England? How did he come here? He's not in the Party."

The woman shook her head.

"It is secret," she replied. "It concerns only the Praesidium. Perhaps the Jew brought him here."

"But *you* know," Liz insisted, a note of blandishment in her voice, "*you* are Commissar at the prison. Surely they told *you*?"

"Perhaps," the woman replied complacently. "It is very secret," she repeated.

The telephone rang. The woman lifted the receiver and listened. After a moment she glanced at Liz.

"Yes, Comrade. At once," she said, and put down the receiver. "You are to stay," she said shortly. "The Praesidium will consider the case of Fiedler. In the meantime you will stay here. That is the wish of Comrade Mundt."

"Who is Mundt?"

The woman looked cunning.

"It is the wish of the Praesidium," she said.

"I don't want to stay," Liz cried. "I want—"

"The Party knows more about us than we know ourselves," the woman interrupted. "You must stay here. It is the Party's wish."

"Who is Mundt?" Liz asked again, but still she did not reply.

Slowly Liz followed her along endless corridors, through grilles manned by sentries, past iron doors from which no sound came, down endless stairs, across whole courtyards far beneath the ground, until she thought she had descended to the bowels of hell itself, and no one would even tell her when Leamas was dead.

She had no idea what time it was when she heard the footsteps in the corridor outside her cell. It could have been five in the evening—it could have been midnight. She had been awake—staring blankly into the pitch-darkness, longing for a sound. She had never imagined that silence could be so terrible. Once she had cried out, and there had been no echo, nothing. Just the memory of her own voice. She had visualized the sound breaking against the solid darkness like a fist against a rock. She had moved her hands about her as she sat on the bed, and it seemed to her that the darkness made them heavy, as if she were groping in the water. She knew the cell was small; that it contained the bed on which she sat, a handbasin without taps, and a crude table: she had seen them when she first entered. Then the light had gone out, and she had run wildly to where she knew the bed had stood, had struck it with her shins, and had remained there, shivering with fright. Until she heard the footstep, and the door of her cell was opened abruptly.

She recognized him at once, although she could only discern his silhouette against the pale blue light in the corridor. The trim, agile figure, the clear line of the cheek and the short fair hair just touched by the light behind him.

"It's Mundt," he said. "Come with me, at once." His voice was contemptuous yet subdued, as if he were not anxious to be overheard.

Liz was suddenly terrified. She remembered the wardress: "Mundt knows what to do with Jews." She stood by the bed, staring at him, not knowing what to do.

"Hurry, you fool." Mundt had stepped forward and seized her wrist. "Hurry." She let herself be drawn into the corridor. Bewildered, she watched Mundt quietly relock the door of her cell. Roughly he took her arm and forced her quickly along the first corridor, half running, half walking. She could hear the distant whirr of air conditioners; and now and then the sound of other footsteps from passages branching from their own. She noticed that Mundt hesitated, drew back even, when they came upon other corridors, would go ahead and confirm that no one was coming, then signal her forward. He seemed to assume that she would follow, that she knew the reason. It was almost as if he were treating her as an accomplice.

And suddenly he had stopped, was thrusting a key into the keyhole of a dingy metal door. She waited, panic-stricken. He pushed the door savagely outwards and the sweet, cold air of a winter's evening blew against her face. He beckoned

to her again, still with the same urgency, and she followed
him down two steps onto a gravel path which led through a
rough kitchen garden.

They followed the path to an elaborate Gothic gateway
which gave on to the road beyond. Parked in the gateway
was a car. Standing beside it was Alec Leamas.

"Keep your distance," Mundt warned her as she started
to move forward. "Wait here."

Mundt went forward alone and for what seemed an age
she watched the two men standing together, talking quietly
between themselves. Her heart was beating madly, her
whole body shivering with cold and fear. Finally Mundt returned.

"Come with me," he said, and led her to where Leamas
stood. The two men looked at one another for a moment.

"Good-bye," said Mundt indifferently. "You're a fool,
Leamas," he added. "She's trash, like Fiedler." And he turned
without another word and walked quickly away into the
twilight.

She put her hand out and touched him, and he half turned
from her, brushing her hand away as he opened the car door.
He nodded to her to get in, but she hesitated.

"Alec," she whispered, "Alec, what are you doing? Why is
he letting you go?"

"Shut up!" Leamas hissed. "Don't even think about it, do
you hear? Get in."

"What was it he said about Fiedler? Alec, why is he letting us go?"

"He's letting us go because we've done our job. Get into
the car; quick!" Under the compulsion of his extraordinary
will she got into the car and closed the door. Leamas got in
beside her.

"What bargain have you struck with him?" she persisted,

suspicion and fear rising in her voice. "They said you had tried to conspire against him, you and Fiedler. Then why is he letting you go?"

Leamas had started the car and was soon driving fast along the narrow road. On either side, bare fields; in the distance, dark monotonous hills were mingling with the gathering darkness. Leamas looked at his watch.

"We're five hours from Berlin," he said. "We've got to make Köpenick by quarter to one. We should do it easily."

For a time Liz said nothing; she stared through the windshield down the empty road, confused and lost in a labyrinth of half-formed thoughts. A full moon had risen and the frost hovered in long shrouds across the fields. They turned onto an autobahn.

"Was I on your conscience, Alec?" she said at last. "Is that why you made Mundt let me go?"

Leamas said nothing.

"You and Mundt are enemies, aren't you?"

Still he said nothing. He was driving fast now, the speedometer showed a hundred and twenty kilometers; the autobahn was pitted and bumpy. He had his headlights on full, she noticed, and didn't bother to dip for oncoming traffic on the other lane. He drove roughly, leaning forward, his elbows almost on the wheel.

"What will happen to Fiedler?" Liz asked suddenly and this time Leamas answered.

"He'll be shot."

"Then why didn't they shoot you?" Liz continued quickly. "You conspired with Fiedler against Mundt, that's what they said. You killed a guard. Why has Mundt let you go?"

"All right!" Leamas shouted suddenly. "I'll tell you. I'll tell you what you were never, never to know, neither you nor I. Listen: Mundt is London's man, their agent; they bought him when he was in England. We are witnessing the lousy end to a filthy, lousy operation to save Mundt's skin. To save him from a clever little Jew in his own Department who had begun to suspect the truth. They made us kill him, do you see, kill the Jew. Now you know, and God help us both."

☒ ☒ 25 ☒ The Wall

"If that is so, Alec," she said at last, "what was my part in all this?" Her voice was quite calm, almost matter-of-fact.

"I can only guess, Liz, from what I know and what Mundt told me before we left. Fiedler suspected Mundt; had suspected him ever since Mundt came back from England; he thought Mundt was playing a double game. He hated him, of course—why shouldn't he—but he was right, too: Mundt was London's man. Fiedler was too powerful for Mundt to eliminate alone, so London decided to do it for him. I can see them working it out, they're so damned academic; I can see them sitting around a fire in one of their smart bloody clubs. They knew it was no good just eliminating Fiedler —he might have told friends, published accusations: they had to eliminate *suspicion*. Public rehabilitation, that's what they organized for Mundt."

He swung into the left-hand lane to overtake a lorry and trailer. As he did so the lorry unexpectedly pulled out in front of him, so that he had to brake violently on the pitted road to avoid being forced into the crash-fence on his left.

"They told me to frame Mundt," he said simply, "they said he had to be killed, and I was game. It was going to be my last job. So I went to seed, and punched the grocer— You know all that."

"And made love?" she asked quietly.

Leamas shook his head. "But this is the point, you see," he continued. "Mundt knew it all, he knew the plan, he had me picked up, he and Fiedler. Then he let Fiedler take over, because he knew in the end Fiedler would hang himself. My job was to let them think what in fact was the truth: that Mundt was a British spy." He hesitated. "Your job was to discredit me. Fiedler was shot and Mundt was saved, mercifully delivered from a fascist plot. It's the old principle of love on the rebound."

"But how could they know about me; how could they know we would come together?" Liz cried. "Heavens above, Alec, can they even tell when people will fall in love?"

"It didn't matter—it didn't depend on that. They chose you because you were young and pretty and in the Party, because they knew you would come to Germany if they rigged an invitation. That man in the Labour Exchange, Pitt, he sent me up there, they knew I'd work at the library. Pitt was in the Service during the war and they squared him, I suppose. They only had to put you and me in contact, even for a day, it didn't matter, then afterwards they could call on you, send you the money, make it look like an affair even if it wasn't, don't you see? Make it look like an infatuation, perhaps. The only material point was that after bringing us together they should send you money as if it came at my request. As it was, we made it very easy for them. . . ."

"Yes, we did." And then she added, "I feel dirty, Alec, as if I'd been put out to stud."

Leamas said nothing.

"Did it ease your Department's conscience at all? Exploiting . . . somebody in the Party, rather than just anybody?" Liz continued.

Leamas said, "Perhaps. They don't really think in those terms. It was an operational convenience."

"I might have stayed in that prison, mightn't I? That's what Mundt wanted, wasn't it? He saw no point in taking the risk—I might have heard too much, guessed too much. After all, Fiedler was innocent, wasn't he? But then he's a Jew," she added excitedly, "so that doesn't matter so much, does it?"

"Oh, for God's sake!" Leamas exclaimed.

"It seems odd that Mundt let me go, all the same—even as part of the bargain with you," she mused. "I'm a risk now, aren't I? When we get back to England, I mean: a Party member knowing all this. . . . It doesn't seem logical that he should let me go."

"I expect," Leamas replied, "he is going to use our escape to demonstrate to the Praesidium that there are other Fiedlers in his Department who must be hunted down."

"And other Jews?"

"It gives him a chance to secure his position," Leamas replied curtly.

"By killing more innocent people? It doesn't seem to worry you much."

"Of course it worries me. It makes me sick with shame and anger and . . . But I've been brought up differently, Liz; I can't see it in black and white. People who play this game take risks. Fiedler lost and Mundt won. London won—that's the point. It was a foul, foul operation. But it's paid off, and that's the only rule." As he spoke his voice rose, until finally he was nearly shouting.

"You're trying to convince yourself," Liz cried. "They've done a wicked thing. How can you kill Fiedler? He was good, Alec; I know he was. And Mundt—"

"What the hell are you complaining about?" Leamas demanded roughly. "Your Party's always at war, isn't it? Sacrificing the individual to the mass. That's what it says. Socialist reality: fighting night and day—the relentless battle—that's what they say, isn't it? At least you've survived. I never heard that Communists preached the sanctity of human life—perhaps I've got it wrong," he added sarcastically. "I agree, yes I agree, you might have been destroyed. That was in the cards. Mundt's a vicious swine; he saw no point in letting you survive. His promise—I suppose he gave a promise to do his best by you—isn't worth a great deal. So you might have died—today, next year or twenty years from now—in a prison in the worker's paradise. And so might I. But I seem to remember the Party is aiming at the destruction of a whole class. Or have I got it wrong?" Extracting a packet of cigarettes from his jacket he handed her two, together with a box of matches. Her fingers trembled as she lit them and passed one back to Leamas.

"You've thought it all out, haven't you?" she asked.

"We happened to fit the mold," Leamas persisted, "and I'm sorry. I'm sorry for the others too—the others who fit the mold. But don't complain about the terms, Liz; they're Party terms. A small price for a big return. One sacrificed for many. It's not pretty, I know, choosing who it'll be—turning the plan into people."

She listened in the darkness, for a moment scarcely conscious of anything except the vanishing road before them, and the numb horror in her mind.

"But they let me love you," she said at last. "And you let me believe in you and love you."

"They used us," Leamas replied pitilessly. "They cheated us both because it was necessary. It was the only way. Fiedler was bloody nearly home already, don't you see? Mundt would have been caught; can't you understand that?"

"How can you turn the world upside down?" Liz shouted suddenly. "Fiedler was kind and decent, he was only doing his job, and now you've killed him. Mundt is a spy and a traitor and you protect him. Mundt is a Nazi, do you know that? He hates Jews. What side are you on? How can you . . . ?"

"There's only one law in this game," Leamas retorted. "Mundt is their man; he gives them what they need. That's easy enough to understand, isn't it? Leninism—the expediency of temporary alliances. What do you think spies are: priests, saints and martyrs? They're a squalid procession of vain fools, traitors too, yes; pansies, sadists and drunkards, people who play cowboys and Indians to brighten their rotten lives. Do you think they sit like monks in London, balancing the rights and wrongs? I'd have killed Mundt if I could, I hate his guts; but not now. It so happens that they need him. They need him so that the great moronic mass you admire can sleep soundly in their beds at night. They need him for the safety of ordinary, crummy people like you and me."

"But what about Fiedler—don't you feel anything for him?"

"This is a war," Leamas replied. "It's graphic and unpleasant because it's fought on a tiny scale, at close range; fought with a wastage of innocent life sometimes, I admit. But it's nothing, nothing at all beside other wars—the last or the next."

"Oh God," said Liz softly. "You don't understand. You don't want to. You're trying to persuade yourself. It's far more terrible, what they are doing; to find the humanity in people, in me and whoever else they use, to turn it like a weapon in their hands, and use it to hurt and kill—"

"Christ Almighty!" Leamas cried "What else have men done. since the world began? I don't believe in anything, don't you see—not even destruction or anarchy. I'm sick, sick of killing but I don't see what else they can do. They don't proselytize; they don't stand in pulpits or on party platforms and tell us to fight for Peace or for God or whatever it is. They're the poor sods who try to keep the preachers from blowing each other sky high."

"You're wrong," Liz declared hopelessly; "they're more wicked than all of us."

"Because I made love to you when you thought I was a tramp?" Leamas asked savagely.

"Because of their contempt," Liz replied; "contempt for what is real and good; contempt for love, contempt for . . ."

"Yes," Leamas agreed, suddenly weary. "That is the price they pay; to despise God and Karl Marx in the same sentence. If that is what you mean."

"It makes you the same," Liz continued; "the same as Mundt and all the rest. . . . I should know, I was the one who was kicked about, wasn't I? By them, by you because you don't care. Only Fiedler didn't. . . . But the rest of you . . . you all treated me as if I was . . . nothing . . . just currency to pay with. . . . You're all the same, Alec."

"Oh Liz," he said desperately, "for God's sake believe me. I hate it, I hate it all, I'm tired. But it's the world, it's mankind that's gone mad. We're a tiny price to pay . . . but everywhere's the same, people cheated and misled, whole lives thrown away, people shot and in prison, whole groups and classes of men written off for nothing. And you, your Party—God knows it was built on the bodies of ordinary people. You've never seen men die as I have, Liz. . . ."

As he spoke Liz remembered the drab prison courtyard, and the wardress saying, "It is a prison for those who slow down the march . . . for those who think they have the right to err."

Leamas was suddenly tense, peering forward through the windshield. In the headlights of the car Liz discerned a figure standing in the road. In his hand was a tiny light which he turned on and off as the car approached. "That's him," Leamas muttered; switched off the headlights and engine, and coasted silently forward. As they drew up, Leamas leaned back and opened the rear door.

Liz did not turn around to look at him as he got in. She was staring stiffly forward, down the street at the falling rain.

"Drive at thirty kilometers," the man said. His voice was taut, frightened. "I'll tell you the way. When we reach the place you must get out and run to the wall. The searchlight will be shining at the point where you must climb. Stand in the beam of the searchlight. When the beam moves away begin to climb. You will have ninety seconds to get over. You go first," he said to Leamas, "and the girl follows. There are iron rungs in the lower part—after that you must pull yourself up as best you can. You'll have to sit on top and pull the girl up. Do you understand?"

"We understand," said Leamas. "How long have we got?"

"If you drive at thirty kilometers we shall be there in about nine minutes. The searchlight will be on the wall at five past one exactly. They can give you ninety seconds. Not more."

"What happens after ninety seconds?" Leamas asked.

"They can only give you ninety seconds," the man repeated; "otherwise it is too dangerous. Only one detachment has been briefed. They think you are being infiltrated into West Berlin. They've been told not to make it too easy. Ninety seconds are enough."

"I bloody well hope so," said Leamas drily. "What time do you make it?"

"I checked my watch with the sergeant in charge of the detachment," the man replied. A light went on and off briefly in the back of the car. "It is twelve forty-eight. We must leave at five to one. Seven minutes to wait."

They sat in total silence save for the rain pattering on the roof. The cobblestone road reached out straight before them, staged by dingy streetlights every hundred meters. There was no one about. Above them the sky was lit with the unnatural glow of arclights. Occasionally the beam of a searchlight flickered overhead, and disappeared. Far to the left Leamas caught sight of a fluctuating light just above the skyline, constantly altering in strength, like the reflection of a fire.

"What's that?" he asked, pointing toward it.

"Information Service," the man replied. "A scaffolding of lights. It flashes news headlines into East Berlin."

"Of course," Leamas muttered. They were very near the end of the road.

"There is no turning back," the man continued. "He told you that? There is no second chance."

"I know," Leamas replied.

"If something goes wrong—if you fall or get hurt—don't turn back. They shoot on sight within the area of the wall. You *must* get over."

"We know," Leamas repeated; "he told me."

"From the moment you get out of the car you are in the area."

"We know. Now shut up," Leamas retorted. And then he added, "Are you taking the car back?"

"As soon as you get out of the car I shall drive it away. It is a danger for me, too," the man replied.

"Too bad," said Leamas drily.

Again there was silence. Then Leamas asked, "Do you have a gun?"

"Yes," said the man, "but I can't give it to you; he said I shouldn't give it to you . . . that you were sure to ask for it."

Leamas laughed quietly. "He would," he said.

Leamas pulled the starter. With a noise that seemed to fill the street the car moved slowly forward.

They had gone about three hundred yards when the man whispered excitedly, "Go right here, then left." They swung into a narrow side street. There were empty market stalls on either side so that the car barely passed between them.

"Left here, now!"

They turned again, fast, this time between two tall buildings into what looked like a cul-de-sac. There was washing strung across the street, and Liz wondered whether they would pass under it. As they approached what seemed to be the dead end the man said, "Left again—follow the path." Leamas mounted the curb, crossed the pavement and they followed a broad footpath bordered by a broken fence to their left, and a tall, windowless building to their right. They heard a shout from somewhere above them, a woman's voice, and Leamas muttered "Oh, shut up" as he steered clumsily around a right-angle bend in the path and came almost immediately upon a major road.

"Which way?" he demanded.

"Straight across—past the chemist—between the chemist and the post office—there!" The man was leaning so far forward that his face was almost level with theirs. He pointed now, reaching past Leamas, the tip of his finger pressed against the windshield.

"Get back," Leamas hissed. "Get your hand away. How the hell can I see if you wave your hand around like that?" Slamming the car into first gear, he drove fast across the wide road. Glancing to his left, he was astonished to glimpse the plump silhouette of the Brandenburg Gate three hundred yards away, and the sinister grouping of military vehicles at the foot of it.

"Where are we going?" asked Leamas suddenly.

"We're nearly there. Go slowly now—left, left, go *left!*" he cried, and Leamas jerked the wheel in the nick of time; they passed under a narrow archway into a courtyard. Half the windows were missing or boarded up; the empty doorways gaped sightlessly at them. At the other end of the yard was an open gateway. "Through there," came the whispered command, urgent in the darkness; "then hard right. You'll see a streetlamp on your right. The one beyond it is broken. When you reach the second lamp, switch off the engine and coast until you see a fire hydrant. That's the place."

"Why the hell didn't you drive yourself?"

"He said you should drive; he said it was safer."

They passed through the gate and turned sharply to the right. They were in a narrow street, pitch-dark.

"Lights out!"

Leamas switched off the car lights, drove slowly forward toward the first streetlamp. Ahead, they could just see the second. It was unlit. Switching off the engine they coasted silently past it, until, twenty yards ahead of them, they discerned the dim outline of the fire hydrant. Leamas braked; the car rolled to a standstill.

"Where are we?" Leamas whispered. "We crossed the Leninallee, didn't we?"

"Greifswalder Strasse. Then we turned north. We're north of Bernauerstrasse."

"Pankow?"

"Just about. Look." The man pointed down a side street to the left. At the far end they saw a brief stretch of wall, gray-brown in the weary arclight. Along the top ran a triple strand of barbed wire.

"How will the girl get over the wire?"

"It is already cut where you climb. There is a small gap. You have one minute to reach the wall. Good-bye."

They got out of the car, all three of them. Leamas took Liz by the arm, and she started from him as if he had hurt her.

"Good-bye," said the German.

Leamas just whispered, "Don't start that car till we're over."

Liz looked at the German for a moment in the pale light: she had a brief impression of a young, anxious face; the face of a boy trying to be brave.

"Good-bye," said Liz. She disengaged her arm and followed Leamas across the road and into the narrow street that led toward the wall.

As they entered the street they heard the car start up behind them, turn and move quickly away in the direction they had come.

"Pull up the ladder, you bastard," Leamas muttered, glancing back at the retreating car.

Liz hardly heard him.

✠ ✠ 26 ✠ In from the Cold

They walked quickly, Leamas glancing over his shoulder from time to time to make sure she was following. As he reached the end of the alley he stopped, drew into the shadow of a doorway and looked at his watch.

"Two minutes," he whispered.

She said nothing. She was staring straight ahead toward the wall, and the black ruins rising behind it.

"Two minutes," Leamas repeated.

Before them was a strip of thirty yards. It followed the wall in both directions. Perhaps seventy yards to their right was a watchtower; the beam of its searchlight played along the strip. The thin rain hung in the air, so that the light from the arc lamps was sallow and chalky, screening the world beyond. There was no one to be seen; not a sound. An empty stage.

The watchtower's searchlight began feeling its way along the wall toward them, hesitant; each time it rested they could see the separate bricks and the careless lines of mortar hastily put on. As they watched the beam stopped immediately in front of them. Leamas looked at his watch.

"Ready?" he asked.

She nodded.

Taking her arm he began walking deliberately across the strip. Liz wanted to run but he held her so tightly that she could not. They were halfway toward the wall now, the brilliant semicircle of light drawing them forward, the beam directly above them. Leamas was determined to keep Liz very close to him, as if he were afraid that Mundt would not keep his word and somehow snatch her away at the last moment.

They were almost at the wall when the beam darted to the north, leaving them momentarily in total darkness. Still holding Liz's arm, Leamas guided her forward blindly, his left hand reaching ahead of him until suddenly he felt the coarse, sharp contact of the cinder brick. Now he could discern the wall and, looking upward, the triple strand of wire and the cruel hooks which held it. Metal wedges, like climbers' pitons, had been driven into the brick. Seizing the highest one, Leamas pulled himself quickly upward until he had reached the top of the wall. He tugged sharply at the lower strand of wire and it came toward him, already cut.

"Come on," he whispered urgently, "start climbing."

Laying himself flat he reached down, grasped her upstretched hand and began drawing her slowly upward as her foot found the first metal rung.

Suddenly the whole world seemed to break into flame; from everywhere, from above and beside them, massive lights converged, bursting upon them with savage accuracy.

Leamas was blinded, he turned his head away, wrenching wildly at Liz's arm. Now she was swinging free; he thought she had slipped and he called frantically, still drawing **her** upwards. He could see nothing—only a mad confusion of color dancing in his eyes.

Then came the hysterical wail of sirens, orders frantically shouted. Half kneeling astride the wall he grasped both her arms in his, and began dragging her to him inch by inch, himself on the verge of falling.

Then they fired—single rounds, three or four, and he felt her shudder. Her thin arms slipped from his hands. He heard a voice in English from the Western side of the wall:

"Jump, Alec! Jump, man!"

Now everyone was shouting, English, French and German mixed; he heard Smiley's voice from quite close:

"The girl, where's the girl?"

Shielding his eyes he looked down at the foot of the wall and at last he managed to see her, lying still. For a moment he hesitated, then quite slowly he climbed back down the same rungs, until he was standing beside her. She was dead; her face was turned away, her black hair drawn across her cheek as if to protect her from the rain.

They seemed to hesitate before firing again; someone shouted an order, and still no one fired. Finally they shot him, two or three shots. He stood glaring around him like a blinded bull in the arena. As he fell, Leamas saw a small car smashed between great lorries, and the children waving cheerfully through the window.